D0569708

DUCKSCARES

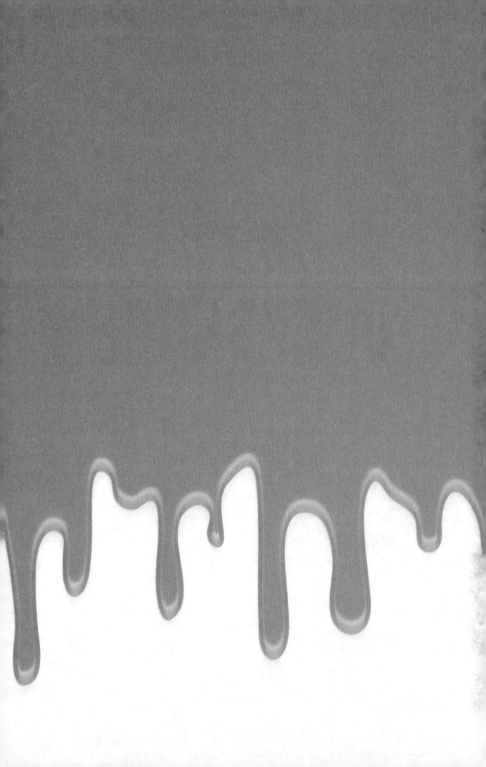

DUCKSCARES

COOKING UP TROUBLE

BY TOMMY GREENWALD

ILLUSTRATED BY ELISA FERRARI

AMULET BOOKS • NEW YORK

Library of Congress Control Number 2021940983

ISBN 978-1-4197-5079-3

© 2021 Disney
Book design by Brenda E. Angelilli and Cheung Tai

Printed and bound in U.S.A.
10 9 8 7 6 5 4 3 2 1

Amulet Books are available at special discounts when purchased
in quantity for premiums and promotions as well as fundraising or
educational use. Special editions can also be created to specification.
For details, contact specialsales@abramsbooks.com or the address below.

Amulet Books® is a registered trademark of Harry N. Abrams, Inc.

ABRAMS The Art of Books
195 Broadway, New York, NY 10007
abramsbooks.com

PROLOGUE

A bolt of lightning cracked and filled the sky above our heads with a bright white light.

"THERE HE IS!" Huey shouted, pointing to the very top of the house. We looked up—**WAY** up—and saw the **SCARY SILHOUETTE** standing on the roof.

He stared down at us on the sidewalk, thrust his cane into the air, and let out a creepy laugh that made all the feathers on the back of my neck stand up.

"AND THERE HE GOES!"

Huey yelled as the shadow leaped from the top of the house to the roof of the building next door.

Then he jumped to the next roof and the next, as easily as jumping over puddles.

"COME ON, GUYS!"

I shouted.

"HE'S GETTING AWAY."

We all took off running in the direction the masked troublemaker was heading. At least, I *THOUGHT* we all took off running.

"WE'VE GOT TO STOP HIM, RIGHT, HUEY?!" I yelled to my left.

"RIGHT!" Huey shouted back.

"RIGHT, LOUIE?"

I shouted, and looked to my right to discover a big empty space where Louie should have been.

Huey and I stopped abruptly, turned around, and saw Louie back where we left him, standing as still as a statue.

We rushed back to him, and Huey asked,

"What's wrong, Louie? We've got to go after him!"

"My mind says 'go,' but my feet say 'no.'"
Louie tugged at his own legs, but his shoes seemed like they were glued to the sidewalk.

"DID YOU STEP IN GUM OR SOMETHING?"
    I asked him.

"NO . . . I think they're scared."

Can you blame them? My feet are used to running AWAY from danger, **not toward it!**

Good point. We're usually getting chased by something . . . It was pretty cool doing the chasing for once!

And think about it, guys. Running after a deranged villain wasn't even the coolest thing we did in Paris! There were hot-air balloon rides, and ghosts galore, and even a werew-

WHOA HUEY!

YOU CAN'T GIVE EVERYTHING AWAY IN THE PROLOGUE.

Then make it snappy and get to Chapter One already!

Louie finally convinced his feet to move by giving them a little pep talk.

You can do this, feet! You got this, toes! Don't make me tickle you!

But by that point, our nemesis had already hopped from roof to roof until he was practically out of sight. We followed him all the way to the center of the city and watched as he did something truly amazing.

He reached the final rooftop, and it looked for a moment like he'd have to turn back or jump down.

But then he took a running start toward the edge of the building and used his cane as if pole-vaulting.

He soared through the air and landed on the side of Paris's most famous landmark:

THE EIFFEL TOWER.

In no time, he climbed all the way to the top and let out the wildest laugh yet. It was one of the most unbelievable things I've ever seen.

If he hadn't been such a terrible, horrifying, monstrous dude, I might have actually been impressed!

As the madman's cackle echoed throughout the city, Louie yelled out, **"Sacrebleu!"** which is French for **"Oh my goodness!"**

He took the words right out of my mouth.

CHAPTER 1

*B*ONJOUR, MES AMIS!

That means "Hello, my friends!" in French.

GUESS WHAT . . . WE'RE IN FRANCE!

That's right, Huey, Dewey, and Louie are taking in the French sights!

They probably figured that out, based on the whole, you know, speaking—French thing.

YEAH, BESIDES, I'M ABOUT TO TELL THEM ALL ABOUT IT!

WELCOME TO PARIS, OTHERWISE KNOWN AS THE CITY OF LIGHTS.

Or in our case, the City of FRIGHTS!

Right. Anyway, when you last saw us, we were saying goodbye to Berlin, Germany, where we'd had the most incredible adventure.

We made lifelong friends, we foiled the evil plan of a vengeful mad scientist, and—the wildest part of all—I ate cabbage!

CABBAGE!!!

Really?
Eating cabbage is wilder
than foiling the plan of a Mad scientist?

YOU'RE RIGHT, HUEY...THEY ARE EQUALLY WILD.

On the flight to Paris, we were feeling nervous for a few reasons.

NUMBER ONE: when we landed, we would meet a whole new group of people, including our French host family.

NUMBER TWO: we were going to a place we'd never been before, which is always a little scary.

And *NUMBER THREE*: Dr. Z, that mad scientist I mentioned a few sentences ago, knew we were going to Paris, and we were afraid he'd follow us there.

So as the plane was landing, Huey, Louie, and I agreed to be brave, think positive, and stick together no matter what. That made us all feel a little bit better. When we got into the airport, we walked around looking for anyone who might be looking for us. There was a big group of people waiting for their friends and family to arrive.

We searched the crowd for someone holding a sign that said **INTERNATIONAL STUDENT AMBASSADORS PROGRAM** (which is the program that made all of this travel possible) or **HUEY, DEWEY, AND LOUIE** or even **NASTY** (which, as you might remember, is the unintentionally hilarious acronym for the **NATIONAL ASSOCIATION OF STUDIOUS AND TALENTED YOUTH**).

But we couldn't find a single person waiting for us.

"NO SIGN? THAT'S A VERY BAD SIGN," Louie said, starting to pace, which he always does when he gets worried, which he always does.

"DON'T WORRY, LOUIE," I told him, pretending to be positive even though I was kind of starting to panic.
"ANY SECOND NOW A NICE PERSON WILL WALK RIGHT UP TO US AND SAY...

"WOUF, WOUF!"

What in the world?! We'd been so busy worrying, we hadn't even noticed that a fluffy white dog with a perfectly round face was staring up at us.

She let out another **"WOUF, WOUF!"** which is French for **"WOOF, WOOF!"**

"**HELLO, GIRL,**" Huey said.

The dog looked at him and cocked her head to one side, confused.

"**I MEAN...BONJOUR, GIRL! WHAT'RE YOU DOING IN THE AIRPORT?**"

Huey reached out to pet the cute pup, and she stepped forward with her chin outstretched. He stroked her head, and her tail wagged back and forth so quickly it made her whole body wiggle. After a minute of petting and wagging and wiggling, the little dog looked up as if she just remembered what she had come inside the airport to do. She grabbed hold of Huey's sleeve with her teeth and began tugging him toward the exit.

"**I THINK SHE WANTS US TO FOLLOW HER.**"

"WOUF, WOUF!" she woofed in agreement, and took off running toward the doors.

We sprinted after her, moving so fast that our wheelie bags barely touched the ground behind us.

"Maybe someone's in trouble!" Huey exclaimed.

"MAYBE SOMEONE NEEDS OUR HELP!" I shouted.

"Maybe someone fell down a well!" Louie yelled.

"A WELL??" Huey and I asked together.

"It happens!"

We kept running, following the white ball of fur as she bolted out of the airport and straight into the arms of a friendly looking man wearing a fancy suit, shiny shoes, and a bow tie.

"Sir, are you in trouble?" Huey exclaimed.

"DO YOU NEED OUR HELP?" I shouted.

"Did you fall down a well?" Louie yelled.

"A WELL??"

The man and the dog looked at Louie and cocked their heads to one side, confused.

"Of course not!" the man said with a big smile.

"Everything is fantastic! We are your host family here in Paris. I am Monsieur Panache, and this is my dog, Cornichon. I sent her inside to greet you!"

"We've never been greeted by a dog before. Best. Welcome. Ever!"

Huey said, high-fiving Louie and me.

"I'm glad you think so," Monsieur Panache said.

"We're so happy you're here. Now let me guess who's who." He took a step back and looked at the three of us, petting Cornichon's head as he thought.

"You must be *Huey*. You must be *DEWEY*. And you must be *Louie*," he said, pointing to each one of us.

And guess what . . . he was right!

"How'd you know?"

Louie asked. "No one can ever tell us apart, let alone guess perfectly on the first try!"

Monsieur Panache looked around to make sure no one was listening, leaned toward us, and whispered, "I'm a little bit *PSYCHIC*."

"NO WAY! REALLY?" I couldn't believe it, and yet I totally believed it. "Yes . . . and your names are writ-

ten on your suitcases," Monsieur Panache said, smiling and looking toward our wheelie bags, which had our names embroidered on the front in big white letters.

How could we forget? Before we left Duckburg, Uncle Donald had our names stitched onto the front pocket of each suitcase, in case we couldn't tell them apart.

As if that could ever happen!

SERIOUSLY! HUEY'S IS RED, MINE IS BLUE, AND LOUIE'S IS . . .

The best color of all: GREEN!

We looked back at Monsieur Panache and all of us started laughing. Even Cornichon looked like she was giggling, and her tongue hung out of the corner of her mouth in the funniest way.

We knew right then that we liked Monsieur Panache. He was nice, he was funny, and he could joke about **PARANORMAL PHENOMENON** like psychic ability.

He was the perfect person to host us!

Plus we couldn't wait to play with Cornichon for three whole months.

We'd never had a pet before . . . unless you count Louie.

That is so not funny.

CHAPTER 2

The very first place we went in Paris was Monsieur Panache's apartment.

That is, if you don't count the airport, which I don't. He and Cornichon lived in a large white building. Outside, it had enormous windows, huge balconies, and big flowerpots.

Inside, it had the world's smallest elevator.

Oh, and P.S.: the elevator wasn't just tiny, but slow, too!

We inched up to the fourth floor, and it was actually a pretty cool experience!

Except for the fact that Huey was standing on my foot the whole time . . .

I was not standing on your foot the whole time! Only for the first three floors . . .

When we finally reached the fourth floor, we spilled into the hallway, where there were seven front doors to choose from.

"Let me guess which one it is," Louie said to Monsieur Panache before beginning to study each door carefully.

"I think it's this one." He pointed to one of the doors.

"How'd you know?" Monsieur Panache asked.

Louie looked around to make sure no one was listening, leaned toward Monsieur Panache, and whispered, **"I'm a little bit psychic."**

"Really?"

"Yes . . . and it's written on your doorbell." Louie said, smiling.

Monsieur Panache laughed and opened the door to his apartment.

"WELCOME HOME, BOYS!"

We stepped through the doorway into a big living room and rushed to the windows to look down at the Parisians walking by.

Question!
If people from Paris are called Parisians, then what are people from Duckburg called?

HMM...DUCKBURGONEMERS?

I like it!

Monsieur Panache and Cornichon showed us the rest of the apartment, including our bedroom, which was awesome, because it had our favorite kind of beds: bunk beds!

"Make yourselves at home, boys!" Monsieur Panache said, holding Cornichon in his arms. "Remember, my raisin is your raisin!"

He did not say "raisin"! He said "maison"!

WHAT'S THE DIFFERENCE?

A maison is a house. A raisin is a grape.

You mean **WAS** a grape.

Just get back to the story.

We decided to take Monsieur Panache's advice and make ourselves at home in our new room.

We unpacked all of our most essential travel items: clothes, toothbrushes, passports, and, of course, **VIDEO GAMES**. (We never go anywhere without them.)

Monsieur Panache put Cornichon down on the ground and looked at the games. He picked one up and turned it over, studying every detail.

At the same time, Cornichon inched over, sniffing one of our controllers with an equal amount of curiosity.

"Wow! I've never played one of these before," Monsieur Panache said. By the time he finished his sentence, our jaws were already on our chests.

Never?

NOT EVEN ONCE??

Are you okay???

"I guess I just never had anyone to play with. Cornichon doesn't have hands, you know? So, do you think you could teach me how?" Monsieur Panache asked.

"Sure! We'd love to!"

Huey answered, but he yawned midway through his sentence, so it sounded more like,

"Sure! Weedlaaauuuvveto!"

His yawn made me yawn, which made Louie yawn, which made Cornichon yawn.

"Gosh, you must be exhausted from your travels, and you have a busy day tomorrow," Monsieur Panache said. "Time for bed, I think."

After we brushed our teeth and put on our pajamas, we said good night to Monsieur Panache and crawled into our awesome bunk beds for a good night's sleep.

"I like Monsieur Panache. Don't you, Dewey?" Huey said to me from the bottom bunk.

"I DO. BUT I CAN'T BELIEVE HE'S NEVER PLAYED A VIDEO GAME BEFORE. CAN YOU, LOUIE?" I said to Louie, up on the top bunk.

"Nope. Meeting someone who's never played a video game before . . . That is probably the weirdest thing that's going to happen to us the whole time we're in Paris!"

We could never have dreamed how wrong that would turn out to be.

CHAPTER 3

I was sleeping like a duckling when all of a sudden the strangest, scariest thing happened!

Without warning, a big, hairy beast jumped on top of me and pinned my shoulders to my bed.

It was enormous and entirely white, like the abominable snowman. I had no idea where it had come from, and I had no time to find out! I yelled for my brothers to help me.

"HUEY, LOUIE, HEEELP!!!
I'M BEING ATTACKED BY A FEROCIOUS BEAST!"

"DEWEY!" I could hear Huey yelling my name, but I couldn't see him anywhere.

"HELP ME, GUYS!" The beast showed its sharp teeth and starting drooling all over my face.

"IT'S TRYING TO EAT ME!"

"DEWEY!" Suddenly, I could hear Louie's voice, too.

"WAAAAKE UUUUUUUP!"

With that, my eyelids popped open, and I was safe in my bunk bed. I had been dreaming . . . or nightmare-ing!

I rubbed my eyes and realized that what I had thought was a fearsome, snarling, abominable beast was actually just friendly, sweet, adorable Cornichon. She was sitting on my chest and gently licking my face.

I rubbed her head and looked at the foot of the bunk beds, where my brothers were staring at me and trying not to laugh.

"Bad dream, Dewey?" Louie asked.

"Careful, Dewey! Cornichon looks hungry." Huey giggled. "Have you had your breakfast yet, Cornichon?"

"Ohhh, breakfast. That's a great idea," I said, eager to change the subject. "Don't try to change the subj—Wait, did you say breakfast?" Louie asked. Lucky for me, my brothers are easily distracted by a lot of things, and breakfast is in the top three. (Lunch and dinner are also in the top three.)

"Good thinking! Come on, Dewey," Huey said.

"Unless you want to stay here alone with that **FEROCIOUS BEAST!**"

They laughed and headed out of our bedroom and toward the kitchen.

I looked at Cornichon, who was still sitting on top of my chest, cocking her head to one side. "I'm sorry I dreamed that you were a big, hairy monster," I told her. "My brothers are never going to let me forget this . . . Now, **THAT'S** a nightmare!"

A little while later, at breakfast, Monsieur Panache asked if we were excited about our first day of school. "New friends, new teachers, new everything!" he said while flipping an omelet over in the frying pan. New friends, new teachers, new, new, new . . . Suddenly, the omelet wasn't the only thing flipping. My stomach felt like it was doing somersaults.

Or cartwheels.

Or a double-twisting double tuck into a triple lay-out with a half twist.

I have no idea what that is . . . but it sounds totally accurate!

By the time we arrived at school, I had butterflies in my belly that were bigger than Cornichon.

We got out of Monsieur Panache's car and started walking toward the entrance, where a boy who looked about our age was bent over, tying his shoe. He looked up, saw us walking in his direction, and let out a big **GASP!** Then he ran inside the school, yelling, *"Allons, allons! They're here!"*

"Do you think we scared him?" I asked.

"Maybe he thought you were the abominable snowman," Huey said, elbowing me in the side.

"Who is *Allons*?" Louie whispered to Monsieur Panache.

"That means 'come on,'" he whispered back, giving Louie a nice reassuring squeeze on the shoulder. "Oh . . ." Louie said. "Then who do you think he was talking to?"

Before Monsieur Panache could answer, a short woman with tall hair burst through the front doors of the school, calling out, "Bonjour! Welcome to Paris!"

She was smiling so much we couldn't help smiling back. Well, Louie and I smiled back.

Huey just stared at her hair, which was a totally uncool thing to do.

I wasn't **STARING!** I was just looking . . . very carefully . . . for a long time . . . without blinking.

Okay, fine, I was staring!

Fortunately, the nice woman didn't seem to notice. "My name is Madame Bouffant," she told us. "I am the principal here at *PARIS'S INTERNATIONAL ELEMENTARY SCHOOL.*"

When he heard the name of the school, Huey stopped staring and started giggling instead. "Otherwise known as *PIES*?" he asked.

Madame Bouffant's already big smile grew even bigger. "We love when people call it that!" she said. "You are very clever. But I wouldn't expect anything less of the International Student Ambassadors. We're so thrilled you're here—which reminds me . . ." She turned back toward the school and yelled cheerily, "*SAMUEL* and *SABINE*! *Allons!*"

On cue, the boy we'd seen tying his shoe ran out the front door of the school beside a girl, and they each carried one end of a long banner.

"A sign! That's a very good sign," Louie said, starting to jump up and down, which he always does when he gets super excited, which he always does.

When the two kids got to where we were standing, they turned the banner over, and it said:

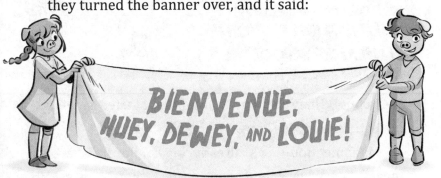

BIENVENUE, HUEY, DEWEY, AND LOUIE!

"'Bienvenue' means 'welcome,'" the boy told us. "I'm Samuel and this is my sister Sabine."

The girl waved with her free hand. "We're in fifth grade, too, and guess what! Madame Bouffant asked us to show you around the school!"

And boy, did they! We saw every inch of **PIES** that day—the classrooms, the library, the playground . . . And we went to a bunch of really cool classes: art, history, and art history (which is kind of like those first two classes smooshed together). Oh, and there were th–

Wait! Tell them what we learned about in history!

UM ... HISTORY?

Be more specific!

French history!

Fine, I'll tell them! We learned about France's most famous King, whose name was ... pausing for suspense ... LOUIE!

Just like ME!

YEAH, BUT HE SPELLED HIS NAME WITH AN "S."

King Souie?

KING LOUIS.

What difference does it make how it's SPELLED? It SOUNDS exactly the same!

YEAH, YOU'RE WRITE.

Huh?

NEVER MIND ... WHERE WAS I?

Oh, and there were these really cool stickers all over the school to help us learn French.

We found out the word for **desk** . . .

and the word for **book** . . .

and the word for **cafeteria**.

THOUGH WE PROBABLY COULD HAVE GUESSED THAT ONE ON OUR OWN.

And we even learned the word for **FRIENDS**.

NEW FRIENDS / NOUVEAUX AMIS

We didn't know how to say "BEST DAY EVER" yet, but that's exactly what it was.

CHAPTER 4

HUEY, LOUIE, AND I DON'T AGREE ABOUT A LOT OF THINGS.

That's not true!

That's not true!

SEE WHAT I MEAN?

But there was one thing we could all agree on: France was **ABSOLUTELY AWESOME!**

Actually, I'd say it was **SERIOUSLY SENSATIONAL!**

No way. . . If you ask me, it was FANTASTICALLY FANTASTIC! FOR REAL!

No matter how you say it, we all **LOVED** Paris. Monsieur Panache  was the greatest host of all time. He told hilarious jokes, he made delicious breakfasts, and he even took us to see an old-timey French movie with English subtitles.

We had read lots of books and seen tons of movies . . .

But this was the first time we had ever READ a MOVIE!

Then there was Cornichon, the cutest dog in the city—no, the world!

She loved to play fetch, she gave the best cuddles, and if anything ever got lost, she could find it in a flash.

Plus we'd been in Paris six whole days, and there had been no sign of Dr. Z. It was great to not have to worry about him after everything that happened in Berlin, at least for a little while. In fact, we hadn't seen a single mad scientist anywhere!

But what we loved most about Paris were our new friends. All the kids in our class were nice and wanted to make us feel welcome, especially Sam and Sabine. They offered to show us around the city and take us to the most renowned attractions. The only problem was we couldn't agree on where to begin.

Wow . . . I guess we really don't agree about most things.

You're right!

CAN WE ALL AGREE THAT THE NEXT PART OF THE STORY GETS REALLY GOOD?

YEP!

YEP!

AND THAT I SHOULD TELL IT RIGHT NOW?

YEP!

YEP!

During our very last class of the week, Sam passed us a note that said: "CIRCLE WHAT YOU WANT TO SEE FIRST."

We didn't really know a lot about any of those things, so we each picked the one that sounded the coolest. I circled the **ARC DE TRIOMPHE**, because it sounded triumphant.

Huey circled the **Eiffel Tower**, because it sounded towering.

And Louie circled the **Louvre** . . .

because it sounded like . . .

pause for suspense . . . **LOUIE!**

We passed the note back to Sam, who stared at it with a stumped look on his face before passing it to Sabine.

When she opened it, we could practically see the light bulb go on above her head.

It was clear she had a great idea.

Finally, the bell rang, at the end of the school day, and it was officially the weekend.

As we packed up our backpacks, Sabine came to our desks with the note in her hand. "Since you can't decide what to see first, we'll have to see everything all at once . . ." Then she whispered something in Sam's ear.

"THAT'S A GREAT IDEA!" Sam shouted. *"Allons! Allons!"* Even though we had no clue what the great idea was, we followed Sam and Sabine as they ran through the hallway of the school, out the front door, and toward the oldest part of the city.

We ran along a big river called the River Seine and waved at the boats floating by.

Hey, what's that supposed to mean?

We ran by a university, passing tons of older students who were carrying books and making serious faces at each other.

Then Huey, Louie, and I saw one of the coolest-looking buildings we'd ever seen in real life, and it stopped us in our tracks. It had enormous columns, a giant dome on the top, and a big carving of what looked like a bunch of people in togas on the front.

"What is this place?" I asked Sam and Sabine.

"It's the **PANTHEON**," Sabine told us.

"We learned all about it in art and history and art history. It was designed to look like a building in Rome. Sometimes Sam and I play on the steps and pretend we're not in Paris at all, but far away in Italy."

"WOW, COOL!" Huey exclaimed. "If you think that's cool, wait until you see . . . everything else! Come on, we're almost there," Sam said, and began running again.

We followed him into a big park filled with trees and flowers and fountains. It was also filled with people who were reading and talking and having picnics in the sunshine.

We had gotten to the center of a big, green field when Sam and Sabine finally stopped running. My brothers and I collapsed onto our backs, trying to catch our breath. "Here it comes!" Sam called out, pointing toward the sky. Huey, Louie, and I looked up, but we couldn't see anything . . . not even a single cloud!

"HERE WHAT COMES?" I asked, but before Sam could answer, I saw it soaring over the horizon.

Turns out, there had been no point in trying to catch our breath anyway, because what happened next totally took our breath away!

CHAPTER 5

Huey, Louie, and I jumped to our feet and watched in disbelief as the biggest thing we'd ever seen flew down from the sky and landed directly on the field in front of us.

It was gigantic; you could stack my brothers and me on each other's shoulders ten times and we still wouldn't be that tall. And it roared so loudly we had to cover our ears. You're probably wondering what it was . . .

Was it a dragon?

NOOO! HUEY, YOU WERE THERE. REMEMBER?

Oh yeah . . . It was a HOT-AIR BALLOON!

DON'T JUST BLURT IT OUT!

You have to pause for suspense!

Even though that's not how I would have said it, Huey's right. It was a humongous hot-air balloon. On the top was the envelope (which is just a fancy word for the balloon part). It was blue, white, and red, because those are the colors of the French flag.

On the bottom was a large basket, kind of like the baskets we saw people using on their picnics, only this one was big enough for all of us to stand in. And in the middle was the burner, which uses gas and fire to fill the balloon with hot air. That's why they call it a hot-air balloon!

The only person allowed to touch the burner was the pilot. His name was **MONSIEUR VOLAND**, but that's

MONSIEUR VOLAND

ENVELOPE

BURNER

BASKET

not what Sam and Sabine called him. They called him **PAPA**.

You see, the pilot was Sam and Sabine's father, and it was his job— his incredible, unbelievable job—to take people on high-flying tours of Paris.

And that day, we were those people!

He helped us all into the basket and turned on the very loud burner. Above our heads, the balloon filled with hot air and stretched until it looked like it might pop. Just when we thought it was ready to burst, the balloon began moving up higher into the sky and lifting the basket off the ground until we were flying through the air! We were soaring abo—

Um, Dewey . . .
Don't you think we ought to tell this part?

Yeah, unless you plan to describe what Paris looked like with your eyes closed.

AW, COME ON, YOU GUYS! EVERYONE ALREADY KNOWS THAT I'M AFRAID OF HEIGHTS. DO YOU HAVE TO KEEP REMINDING THEM?

No, we don't have to keep reminding them.

We just have to make sure no one ever forgets.

FIIINE. YOU CAN TELL THIS PART, BUT I'M COVERING MY EARS THIS TIME!

SWEEEEET! Get ready, everybody. This book is about to get even more AWESOME.

We are WAY better narrators than Dewey. Right, Dewey?

WHAAAT?!?!
I CAN'T HEAR YOU.

CHAPTER

6

Welcome to the super-spectacular sixth chapter, brought to you by Huey and Louie!

There we were, soaring above the park and waving down at the people who were reading and talking and having picnics in the sunshine. **"See?** Now you don't have to decide what to see first!" Sabine said.

"You'll get a bird's-eye view of the whole city!" Sam added. **And they were right!** Before we knew it, we were flying above the biggest art museum in the world: **The LOUVRE.**

It's famous for a lot of things, like giant statues and a much less giant painting on the inside, and there is even a bakery with THE BEST RAISIN croissants in the entire world.

Next we zoomed over the top of the Arc de Triomphe, which is a massive monument at the center of twelve busy streets. A monument is kind of like a statue, only bigger, and the Arc de Triomphe is the second-most-popular monument in all of Paris.

Sort of like Dewey, the second-most-popular brother in all of Duckburg!

WAIT A MINUTE! I AM NOT SECOND MOST POPULAR.

I thought you weren't listening.

I WASN'T. I MEAN... I'M NOT. KEEP GOING!

Finally, we flew all the way to the Eiffel Tower, the MOST popular monument in all of Paris!

Sort of like me, the MOST popular brother in all of Duckburg!

You mean ME?

CALL IT A TIE?

Deal! It's still better than second.

I HEARD THAT!

We had seen the Eiffel Tower plenty of times before. . . in movies, in books, on postcards, and on magnets!

But we couldn't believe we were finally seeing it in person with our very own eyes. Well, WE were seeing it. Dewey was busy memorizing the insides of his eyelids.

Monsieur Voland maneuvered the hot-air balloon directly next to the tower and said, "Want to know something cool? The Eiffel Tower is made entirely of strong, sturdy iron. But it can still sway two to three inches on very windy days. The other hot-air balloon pilots and I have a little saying: If the Eiffel Tower is a'swaying, on the ground we'll be staying."

Suddenly, Sam and Sabine started shouting excitedly. "Look! look! There's our favorite place in all of Paris: La Premiere Pâtisserie!" they said, pointing to a shop with a royal-blue awning below us.

"What's a Pâtisserie?" Louie asked.

"It's a bakery!" Sabine replied.

"It's not just A bakery," Sam said. "It's the BEST bakery! And I'm not only saying that because we're pretty much BFFs with the owner."

"Her name is Christine LeBlanc. She makes the most incredible pastries you've ever seen or smelled or, most importantly, tasted. We help her in the bakery all the time!" Sabine added.

THEN, THE WEATHER TOOK AN UNEXPECTED TURN.

Dewey! Don't steal our thunder.

Or our lightning!

SORRY, I'M JUST SO USED TO NARRATING! GO AHEAD. YOU GUYS ARE DOING A GREAT JOB!

In seconds, the sky went from bright and sunny to dark and cloudy. "Look at that," Sabine said, pointing to the Eiffel Tower, which was swaying in the wind, just like Monsieur Voland told us it could.

"I'm sorry, kids," he said as thunder roared in the distance. "A storm is coming. These flying conditions are not good." It turns out "NOT GOOD" is NOT a phrase you want to hear from your hot-air balloon pilot.

"Don't worry," he said, which was totally worrying. "We'll be fine just as long as we don't get hit by a big gust of wind!"

And then **WHOOOOOOOOSH!** Just as he said that, a big gust of wind hit the balloon and propelled us to the left. We held on tight to the basket to keep from falling over the side.

"Don't worry," Monsieur Voland said again, even though we were already EXTREMELY worried. "We"ll be fine just as long as we don't get hit by an even **BIGGER** gust of wind!"

Just as he said that, an even **BIGGER** gust of wind—a gust of wind so big we thought it might knock the Eiffel Tower all the way over—hit the balloon. It whipped us to the right and zipped us to the left. We've never been inside a hurricane, but now we know how it feels!

"Uh-oh," Monsieur Voland said, looking at a rope that connected one corner of the basket to the envelope (you know, the balloon part). It turns out "Uh-oh," is **ALSO** not something you want to hear from your hot-air balloon pilot. All the whipping and zipping was making the rope unravel. Any second, it would **SNAP!**

Then it happened! The rope gave way, and Monsieur Voland dove forward to catch it. Sam and Sabine grabbed his legs to keep him from flying into the air or tumbling over the side of the basket.

"We've got to land!" Monsieur Voland shouted. "Huey, Dewey, and Louie, you have to turn down the burner. The hot air is making the balloon go up. If you turn down the burner, it will go down!"

"But we can't!" Huey protested.

"You have to! If Sam and Sabine let go of me, I'll lose hold of this rope. If I lose hold of this rope, the basket will tip over. It's up to you!" Monsieur Voland shouted back.

"But we're not allowed to touch the burner, remember?" Louie reminded him. (Though the truth is we had been desperate to touch the burner ever since Monsieur Voland said we weren't allowed to!)

"You have my permission. But hurry!"

So we did! We stretched for the burner, but it was way too high for the average twelve-year-old to reach. And even though we're above average in looks and brains and courage...

DO YOU THINK ANYONE IS STILL READING THIS?

...we are totally average in terms of height.

We tried everything. We stood on our tiptoes. We stretched as far as our arms would stretch. We jumped as high as we could jump.

"It's no use!" I cried out.

"We could stand on each other's shoulders and we still wouldn't be tall enough!" I said, dismayed. "Unless . . ." We both looked over at Dewey, though he didn't know that, because his eyes were still sealed shut.

"UNLESS WHAT???" He said.

"Dewey, you've got to help us!"

We answered.

"HOW CAN I HELP YOU? I CAN'T EVEN SEE YOU!" Dewey replied as the balloon continued careening out of control. *"AND I'M TOO SCARED!"*

"Come on, dude," I said. "You've got to open your eyes! I think it's time for one of my pep talks!"

I cracked my knuckles and grabbed Dewey by the shoulders. "Dewey, remember in Berlin how you faced your fear of snakes? And how you escaped from that green goblin? And how you helped capture Dr. Z? If you can do all of THAT, you can do THIS!"

Dewey thought about how totally terrifying all those things had been. Every single one of them had scared the bejeepers out of him! But even though they scared him, they never stopped him. Dewey took a deep breath, gathered all the courage he could muster, annnnnnd
. . . pause for suspense . . .

OPENED MY EYES!
OKAY, YOU GUYS. I CAN TAKE IT FROM HERE!

CHAPTER
7

Welcome to the super-DUPER, even more spectac-
ular seventh chapter, brought to you by your trusty
narrator ... *ME, DEWEY!!*

Like my brothers were saying, things in the hot-air
balloon were getting hairy ... and *FAST.*

When I opened my eyes, I finally saw what was
happening in the basket: Monsieur Voland was
holding on to a piece of frayed rope, Sam and Sabine
were holding on to Monsieur Voland, and Huey and
Louie were holding on to each other. They looked
totally freaked out!

Because we WERE totally freaked out!

Yes, BUT we had a plan.

"To reach the burner, we've got to be a lot taller," Huey explained.

"So we all have to stand on each other's shoulders," Louie added.

"Got it!" I said. "We'll stack ourselves up like blocks! **OR PANCAKES!**"

I should have known better than to mention pancakes.

They fall into the "breakfast food" category, and we all know how easily my brothers get distracted by breakfast.

"Oooh, pancakes!" Huey started licking his lips.

"I looove pancakes!" Louie began rubbing his tummy.

"If we don't hurry, we'll all be **FLAT AS PANCAKES!**" I shouted. "Come on, let's stack!"

Huey stayed on the bottom, because he has strong arms; Louie climbed on top of Huey's shoulders, because he has great balance; and I climbed on top of Louie's shoulders, which made me just tall enough to reach the burner.

I turned the nozzle to the right, and the medium-sized flame grew into a mega-sized flame, sending us flying even higher into the air.

"TO THE LEFT, DEWEY!" Monsieur Voland cried out. I could see that he was starting to lose his grip on the rope.

I turned the nozzle to the left, and the mega-sized flame shrunk into a medium-sized flame and then a mini-sized flame. As the flame got smaller, the balloon began floating toward the ground. In no time, we were low enough that the wind couldn't whip us around anymore.

I jumped off Louie's shoulders, and he jumped off Huey's shoulders, and we all held on tight as the balloon got closer and closer to the ground.

We were headed for a big field right beside the Eiffel Tower. We found out later it's called the Parc du Champ-de-Mars. As we came in for a landing, the bottom of the basket just missed some kids playing tag.

You mean some dudes playing Frisbee?

Yep, that's what I meant!

Okay, I have a little confession... the landing part was just as scary as the flying part. And I kind of closed my eyes again. But don't tell my brothers!

Don't tell us what?

Nothing! Where was I?

When the basket finally touched down, I was so happy to be out of the sky that I practically dove onto the field. And I wasn't the only one! Everyone jumped out of the basket and joined me in the grass.

I was just getting used to the feeling of solid ground beneath my feet when all of a sudden I was in the air again. Monsieur Voland had scooped me up, along with Huey and Louie, and was giving us all a big hug.

"Thank you, boys! I don't know how I can ever repay you!" he cried.

"You don't have to repay us," I told him. "But could you please put us back on the ground?"

Monsieur Voland laughed and put us down next to Sam and Sabine, who were high-fiving each other and cheering for us!

"You did it! Hooray for the INTERNATIONAL STUDENT HEROES!"

Being a hero makes you feel a lot of things. I felt cool and courageous!

I FELT FEARLESS AND FIRED UP!

I just felt jealous.

JEALOUS???

Yep. Jealous. Because I wanted to turn down the burner.

Don't worry, Louie.
You can turn down the burner next time!

NEXT TIME?!?!

CHAPTER

8

Like I was saying, being a hero makes you feel
a lot of things. But mostly, it makes you feel hungry!
After celebrating our heroicness for a while, we sat
in the grass with Sam and Sabine, watching Monsieur
Voland repair his hot-air balloon and listening to our
stomachs growling.

Monsieur Voland must have heard them, too,
because he suggested that we all go to La Première
Pâtisserie for a well-deserved treat.

All we could see from
the air was the royal blue
awning, but when we
reached the bakery, we
realized that there was so
much more to see inside!

There was a glass case that ran from one end of the bakery to the other, and it was filled with rows and rows of every kind of yummy thing you could imagine: loaves of piping hot bread, buttery croissants fresh from the oven, enormous éclairs overflowing with frosting . . .

Dewey, you're drooling.

WHOOPS! WHERE WAS I?

There were cakes covered in powdered sugar, cups of creamy chocolate mousse, tarts topped with fresh strawberries, blueberries, raspberries . . .

Still drooling.

I can't help it!
It was totall drool-worthy.

Sam and Sabine were showing Huey and Louie which of the tarts they liked best, but I wasn't listening. I was too busy staring at a sandwich-slash-bun-slash-croissant that was unlike anything I'd ever seen before.

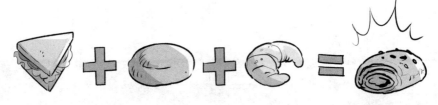

I pressed my beak against the case, trying to get a closer look, when all of a sudden a face appeared on the other side of the glass.

"Boo!" the face said, which made me jump back so quickly I almost knocked over a display of colorful cookies.

Almost? You totally knocked it over.

"Whoops! I didn't mean to startle you." I saw then that the face belonged to a woman, who giggled in my direction. Her long blond hair was pulled back in a low ponytail, and she wore a white chef's hat that matched her white apron.

"Welcome to my bakery!" the woman said with a friendly smile.

"Are you Madame LeBlanc?" I asked.

"*Oui!*" she replied. "But you can call me Christine. All my favorite customers do. Isn't that right, Sam and Sabine?" Sam and Sabine were picking up the colorful cookies off the floor. They called out, "*Oui*, Christine!"

Now would be a good time to tell you that "**OUI**" sounds like "**WE**."

It's the French word for "YES." We heard it a lot while we were in Paris.

OUI, we did.

I introduced myself. "I'm Dewey, and these are my brothers, Huey and Louie. We're the Internatio–" "*THE INTERNATIONAL STUDENT AMBASSADORS!*" Christine chimed in before I could finish. "I've heard so much about you from Sam and Sabine. They're always talking about their cool new friends from America."

I was sure my cheeks were turning as red as the strawberries on top of the tarts. I looked at Sam and Sabine, and they were blushing, too.

"It's great to meet you! I saw you checking out the *pain au chocolat*. Would you like to try one?" Christine pointed inside the glass case at the sandwich-slash-bun-slash-croissant things.

"Sure!" I said excitedly. "But . . . what is it?"

"*'Pain'* means 'bread' and *'chocolat'* means 'chocolate.' It's chocolate bread!" she told us.

"I love bread!" Huey said.

"And I love chocolate!" Louie said.

"And I have a feeling I'm going to love chocolate bread!" I said.

"I'm sure you will! We should make a fresh batch." Christine gestured to the far end of the bakery and told us to follow her into the kitchen.

Her kitchen made our kitchen at home look like a toy! Pots and pans hung from the ceiling above the sparkling silver countertops and there were at least five ovens.

Right away, Sam and Sabine ran into a pantry and started grabbing bowls and mixers and ingredients off the shelves.

"Sam and Sabine are very good bakers! We make an awesome team," Christine said, looking at them proudly.

And she was right! The three of them worked together like a great jazz trio or a Division I basketball

team, depending on whether you prefer music or sports. Sam mixed and blended the ingredients.

Sabine chopped the chocolate and put the pieces inside the dough.

Christine prepared the trays and turned on the oven.

Plus, she snuck my brothers and me a few pieces of chocolate to taste while we waited.

MM MM *MMMM!*

And all the while, she told us about the history of the bakery.

"Over one hundred years ago, the most renowned baker in all of Paris opened La Première Pâtisserie. His name was **MONSIEUR ERIK LEROUX.**" She pointed behind her, where a painting of Monsieur Leroux was hanging on the wall next to a rack of rolling pins. I didn't know why, but looking at that painting gave me goose bumps all over my body.

You mean duck bumps.

EXACTLY!

Christine put the freshly rolled chocolate bread in the oven, set a timer, and went on with the story.

"Monsieur Leroux spent his life perfecting each one of his recipes, and he put them all in this book." Below the painting was a shelf with a single book on it. Christine took it down, and we could see that it was very, very old.

It was even more ancient than Uncle Donald!

EXACTLY!

"When Monsieur Leroux died, he passed the bakery and his beloved book of recipes on to his apprentice, who passed them on to his apprentice, who passed them on to her apprentice, until just one year ago, when they were passed on to me! And one day, I'll pass them on to my own little apprentices. Isn't that right, Sam and Sabine?"

"*Oui*, Christine!" they answered. "But when will you teach us to make Leroux's famous crème brûlée?" Sabine asked, flipping to that recipe in the book.

"Yes, we want to use the sugar torch!" Sam exclaimed. Christine smiled and said, "Remember, one of the most important parts of baking is patience. You've mastered *pain au chocolat*. Tomorrow we'll make some macarons. And soon I'll teach you crème brûlée." She closed the book and handed it to Sam.

"Now hurry and put the book back on the shelf– unless you want a visit from . . . **LE FANTÔME!**" she said in a spooky voice that gave my duck bumps duck bumps!

"Chriiiistine." Sam rolled his eyes as he put the book back on the shelf.

"There's no such thing as le Fantôme."

"'Fantôme' sounds an awful lot like the English word for 'phantom,'" Louie said, looking leery. "So, what does it mean?"

PLEASE DON'T SAY "PHANTOM." PLEASE DON'T SAY "PHANTOM" . . .

"It means 'phantom,'" Sabine replied.

"What's a phantom?" Huey asked.

"A phantom is a GHOST. It's usually the spirit of someone from long ago. And legend has it there used to be one in this very bakery," Christine explained in a hushed voice.

An eerie silence fell over the kitchen. It was so quiet you could hear a *pain au chocolat* drop.

DIIIING!

The timer **DINGED**, breaking the silence and scaring the crème brûlée out of us.

In fact, it made Louie jump back so quickly he almost knocked over the rack of rolling pins.

ALMOOOST?!?!

CHAPTER 9

*H*ave you ever tried to walk on rolling pins?

I do not recommend it! It's like trying to in-line skate on top of a trampoline on top of a treadmill—which actually sounds kind of fun but would be really hard! It took forever to clean up the rolling pins, but when we'd returned all of them to the rack, we finally got to try the *pain au chocolat*.

And let me tell you, chocolate bread is without question...

THE BEST THING WE'VE EVER TASTED!

THE BEST THING WE'VE EVER TASTED!

THE BEST THING WE'VE EVER TASTED!

Just as we were savoring the last sweet, buttery bites, Christine said it was time to close for the day. "But please come back tomorrow after school. Sam, Sabine, and I will bake you some fresh macarons!"

Macarons are those colorful cookies Dewey mentioned earlier.

Remember? The ones he knocked all over the floor.

YOU GUUUUYS, MACARONS ARE NOT AN IMPORTANT PART OF THE PLOT.

But they ARE delicious!

How do you know that?

On second thought, Dewey's right. They're not an important part of the plot. Forget I said anything!

YOU ATE ONE OFF THE FLOOR, DIDN'T YOU?

Maybe... five-second rule!

That is so disturbing.

BUT NOT AS DISTURBING AS WHAT HAPPENED NEXT!

At school the next day, pastries were all I could think about! During art, I drew pictures of tarts. During history, I daydreamed about croissants.

During art history, I imagined a mash-up of a tart and a croissant, called a *troissart*.

And when I wasn't thinking about pastries, I was thinking about the Phantom...

We had to know the whole story. After all, creepy things are our thing!

We thought we could find out more about le Fantôme when we went back to the bakery after school.

And boy, were we right.

When the final bell rang, we ran with Sam and Sabine as fast as our legs would go, but when we got to the bakery, we found something strange: there was a large sign on the door that said *fermé*.

"What does *fermé* mean?" Louie asked Sam and Sabine.

"Closed," Sabine answered with a confused look on her face. "But that's weird. Christine would never close the bakery this time of day. Something must be wrong."

"Wow," Louie said. "Usually a sign is a good sign. But this seems like a very bad sign."

"I have an idea!" Sam cried out. "We can go around to the back, where Christine always keeps a kitchen window open. Sometimes, Sabine and I stand back there and play a game where we try to guess what Christine is baking based only on the smell."

We followed Sam and Sabine to the back of the bakery, where a window was cracked open just enough that we could squeeze through.

Once all five of us were in the kitchen, we couldn't believe our eyes.

The pots and pans that had been hanging from the ceiling were thrown all

over the floor. There were bowls of flour and powdered sugar overturned on the once-sparkling silver counter-tops. And all five of the oven doors were left wide open.

"Something is definitely wrong," Sabine said with a concerned look on her face.

Then we heard it: someone was banging around in the pantry!

SBANG!

SBONG!

"Christine!" Sam cried out gleefully, running toward the noise.

"Wait, Sam! **DON'T!**" But before Sabine could stop him, Sam pulled open the pantry door.

A cloud of sugar, salt, and flour burst into the kitchen, and in the very center of it was a man—or what looked like a man—in a black chef's hat and a black apron.

He wore an all-black suit with a black cape.

And if that outfit wasn't already freaky enough, he also wore a **MASK** that covered the top half of his face. Guess what color it was! RED! (I bet you thought I was going to say black.)

"Le Fantôme . . ." Sabine whispered, and the man—or whatever he was—let out a laugh so loud it shook the rack of rolling pins, sending a few flying onto the floor.

"WHAT DO YOU WANT?" I shouted.
"WHAT ARE YOU DOING HERE?" Huey hollered.

"WHERE'S CHRISTINE?"

Louie screamed.

We could see the Phantom's pitch-black eyes through the small holes of his mask, and he was staring right at us.

Without moving, he looked to the right, and the oven doors **SLAMMED SHUT.**

WE WERE TRAPPED! AND WHAT'S WORSE, THE PHANTOM HAD BEGUN WALKING TOWARD US.

This part was so awfully scary!

This part was so awesomely scary!

Then he looked to the left, and the overturned bowls cracked and broke into pieces on the counter. All five of us took off running back toward the open window, but he flung out his arm and it slammed shut.

They're both right.

It was awfully, awesomely scary.

We stood beneath the closed window as the Phantom inched closer and closer.

And just when we thought he couldn't seem any more **SINISTER**, he spoke:

"I'LL BURN YOU AND YOUR PAIN AU CHOCOLAT TILL THE BOTTOMS ARE BLACK. GET AWAY FROM THIS BAKERY AND NEVER COME BACK."

He took one more step in our direction, and just when we thought we were goners, he put his foot down right on top of a rolling pin.

Remember, **I DO NOT** recommend trying to walk on rolling pins!

The Phantom slipped and flew backwards onto the ground, giving us just enough time to escape from the kitchen, run through the bakery, sprint past the long glass case, and bolt out the front door.

We could hear the Phantom shouting at us from the doorway, but we didn't turn back to look.

We had seen enough of that guy for one day!

CHAPTER
10

I've seen some very scary things before, like the cage full of creepy spiders Dr. Z unleashed on us in his laboratory . . . and the giant snake monster he sent chasing us down the street . . . and Huey's feathers when he first wakes up in the morning!

Oh, like yours is any better!

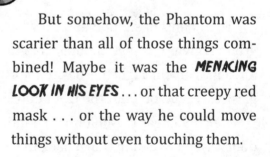

But somehow, the Phantom was scarier than all of those things combined! Maybe it was the **MENACING LOOK IN HIS EYES** . . . or that creepy red mask . . . or the way he could move things without even touching them.

That's called telekinesis.

TELEKI-WHAT, BRO?

Telekinesis! It's the ability
to move an object with your mind.

WHAT ARE YOU DOING?

I'm trying to use my mind
to MOVE the story along.

After we hightailed it from the bakery, we followed Sam and Sabine all the way to Christine's house. We had to make sure she was okay!

We turned onto her street and saw three tall, skinny houses in a row.

They were identical in every way except for the front doors, which were red, blue, and green.

They were triplets . . . house triplets! And, of course, Christine's door was the best color of all: *BLUE!*

Um, Dewey, we already established way back in chapter one that **GREEN** is the best color.

We did NOT!
RED is clearly the best color.

STOMP!

OKAY, THAT'S IT! THE NEXT PERSON WHO INTERRUPTS THE STORY OWES ME AN ORANGE SODA!

As I was saying, Sam and Sabine darted up to the **BLUE** door and knocked, but there was no answer. They knocked again, a little louder this time, but there was still no answer.

Just as Sabine was about to begin knocking for a third time, Sam turned to her and said, "**THE KEY!** Christine once told us that she hides a spare key in her front yard. Let's look for it!"

So we did. Sam looked under some rocks, Sabine looked beneath the mailbox, and Louie looked above the doorframe. Meanwhile, I was looking at Louie, who had gotten distracted (surprise, surprise) by a small garden gnome.

It was just like the ones we have in our yard at home, except this gnome didn't wear a tall pointy hat.

He wore a beret, which is a kind of hat invented in France! Do you guys think I would look good in a beret? I've always wanted to wear one, but I worry that my head is too flat. What? Why are you looking at me like that??

YOU OWE ME
AN ORANGE SODA . . .

Aw, man! Me and my big
mouth and my flat head . . .
But seriously, do you think
I'd look good in a beret?

Huey picked up the gnome off the ground. "Bonjour, little gnome!"

"Huey, do you have to touch **EVERYTHING??**" I asked him, rolling my eyes. "Put that down!"

"**Fiiiiine . . .**" he said, rolling his eyes back at me.

But when he started to put the gnome back on the ground, the gnome's beret flew off his head and landed deep in a flower bed.

"Great job, Huey!" Louie said sarcastically. "You lost his hat!" Huey didn't respond at first. He just looked at the top of the gnome's now bare head. "You're right. I lost his hat. But I foooound"—he paused for suspense—" . . . the **KEY!**"

Huey held out the gnome, and there, taped to the top of his head, was a door key.

"GREAT JOB, HUEY!"

Louie said, only this time, he wasn't being sarcastic.

Sabine used the key to open the front door. Once all five of us were inside, we couldn't believe our eyes. It was a complete mess, just like the bakery. In the front hall, there were papers and pieces of mail scattered all over the place.

As we got into the living room, we saw that every book from Christine's bookshelf had been thrown onto the floor. And in the kitchen—which looked like a shrunken-down version of the kitchen at La Première Pâtisserie—everything appeared out of place.

"It looks like the Phantom has been here, too," said Sabine.

The expression on her face was getting more and more concerned every second.

"Let's just hope he's not *STILL* here," Huey said.

Then we heard it: someone was banging around in the pantry.

"Christine!" Sam cried out gleefully, running toward the noise.

"Wait, Sam! **DON'T!**" But before Sabine could stop him, Sam pulled open the pantry door.

Whoa, I am having some serious deja vu.

Same! Only spooky.

Déjà BOO!

Nice one!

We held our breath and closed our eyes, waiting for the Phantom to burst out of the pantry in a cloud of sugar, salt, and flour, just like he'd done at the bakery. But there was no bursting. No cloud. No nothing!

We opened our eyes and peered into the pantry to see who was making all that noise.

And you'll never believe it . . . it was *CHRISTINE!*

She was frantically searching the shelves for something, but we didn't know what.

"Christine!" Sam cried out even more gleefully, running toward her.

She turned around and seemed just as surprised to see us as we'd been to see her. "Kids! What are you doing here? How did you get in?"

We had SO much to tell her and SO much to ask her, SO we did it all at once!

"Come, sit down. I'll explain everything!" Christine led us into her living room and we took a seat on the sofa. She put a plate of cookies that looked like seashells 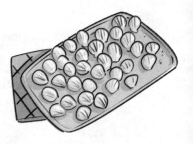 on the coffee table in front of us and said, "These are called madeleines. Bon appétit."

"What does 'bon appétit' mean?" Louie asked.

"It's kind of like saying 'eat up,'" she explained.

"Oh. No thanks, Christine. I'm not hungry . . ." Louie said. Then his eyes got wide. "Wow, I've never felt this way before."

"That's okay, Louie. I've lost my appetite, too."

Christine plopped down in the chair across from us and started to explain everything. "I was in the kitchen at La Première Pâtisserie. I was about to start a fresh batch of macarons when I heard something strange . . . a voice behind me whispering, '*Le livre.*'"

LE LIVRE

"*Livre* ... that means 'book!'" Huey chimed in proudly.

"That's right!" Christine said, smiling at Huey, even though I'm sure she didn't feel much like smiling. "Then I heard the voice again, only louder this time. It said, '*Où est le livre?*'"

"That means 'Where is the book?'" Sabine told us.

"Then I turned around, and standing right behind me was ..."

"*Oui!* He was staring at me through that creepy red mask and pointing at the shelf on the wall.

I looked at it, and Leroux's recipe book was **GONE!** Then pots and pans began falling on the floor, and the oven doors slammed open, but the Phantom never moved!

"I ran from the bakery all the way home without ever looking back," Christine said.

"So . . ." Louie looked at Christine and asked the question that was on all our minds. "*Où est le livre?*"

"Where is the book? I wish I knew!" Christine threw up her hands. "I know I had it the day we baked the *pain au chocolat.* And I thought I might have brought it home, but I've looked everywhere. That's why it's such a mess in here. I must have lost it someplace, and now I don't know what to do!"

We were all quiet for a moment, and then Huey said, "Whenever I lose something, Uncle Donald says . . . "

"Retrace my steps . . . "
Christine said, considering it. "That's not a bad idea!"

CHAPTER

11

We decided to put Huey's "not bad" idea into action!

The next day, we would go everywhere Christine had gone after baking the *pain au chocolat* for us. She made a list of locations and we decided to split up so we could cover more ground!

Sam and Sabine volunteered to visit the dog groomer. Christine said she'd search along the River Seine. And my brothers and I offered to check out the *fromagerie* (even though we had no clue what a *fromagerie* was).

EVERYWHERE
CHRISTINE WENT

1) Delivered pet-friendly pastries to the Barc de Triomphe Dog Groomer

2) Strolled along the River Seine

3) Dropped off baguettes at François's Fromagerie

The following morning, we woke up raring to go! But before we started our investigation, Monsieur Panache insisted that we have the "most important meal of the day." Personally, I think all meals are equally important—including the meals we have between meals—but I've never said no to breakfast!

Monsieur Panache made us three of his signature omelets, and after we'd practically licked our plates clean, we were ready to get started! Actually, Louie and I were ready. Huey, on the other hand, had lost his hat. We knew exactly what Uncle Donald would say . . .

NOT **AGAIN**, HUEY! YOU WOULD LOSE YOUR BEAK IF IT WEREN'T STUCK TO YOUR FACE! YOU SHOULD RETRACE YOUR STEPS.

But you know what's better—and faster—than retracing your steps? Cornichon! Remember if, anything ever went missing, she could find it in a flash.

She sniffed Huey's clothes and set off in search of the missing hat. Her nose led her into our bedroom, and in no time, she found his hat tucked under a pile of clothes.

Huey took his hat from Cornichon's mouth. "Thank you, Cornichon! You can find anything, can't you, girl?"

That gave me an idea, so I said, "That gives me an idea! Maybe Cornichon can help find Monsieur Leroux's missing recipe book."

"Good thinking!" Louie exclaimed. "Can she come with us, Monsieur Panache?"

"I don't mind! But it's up to her." Monsieur Panache looked at Cornichon and asked, "Would you like to go with Huey, Dewey, and Louie today?"

"WOUF, WOUF!" she woofed in agreement.

"Yippee!" I cheered. "Off to the *fromagerie!*"

"Oh, you're going to the cheese shop! Send my best wishes to the owner, François," Monsieur Panache said before heading back into the kitchen.

"Did you hear that, guys? A *fromagerie* is a cheese shop," I said excitedly. I don't like to brag, but I'm kind of an expert when it comes to cheese. I've tried all kinds—cheddar, Swiss, mozzarella, and my personal favorite: grilled.

CHEDDAR   **MOZZARELLA**

SWISS   **GRILLED**

But the *fromagerie* took my breath away. It had more cheeses than I even knew existed! And it was very . . . well . . . **STINKY!**

It smelled . . .

Funnnnnnky

As soon as we walked in, Cornichon trotted over to a friendly-looking man who was arranging samples on a tray beneath a big blackboard that listed every kind of cheese in the shop.

"WOUF, WOUF!" she woofed up at him.

"Bonjour, Cornichon!" He smiled and turned to us. "Bonjour, boys! I'm François. Are you looking for some cheese?"

"Actually, we're looking for a book," Louie replied.

"Then you don't want a *fromagerie*. You want a *bibliothèque*!" François let out a big belly laugh.

"What does '*bibliothèque*' mean?" Louie asked.

"'Library,'" François answered.

"I'm sure you can find at least one book there!" He let out another belly-shaking laugh, but we had no time for **CHEESY** jokes!

We told him about everything that had happened to us over the last few days: meeting Christine, trying *pain au chocolate*, coming face to masked face with the Phantom. When we got to the last part, though, François had an unexpected reaction. He didn't gasp or groan or get freaked out at all.

He started giggling, and his giggling grew until he was full-on guffawing!

After a few moments, François stopped and said, "Forgive me, boys. It's just that I know all about *le Fantôme*. My father used to tell me that story when I was your age. Have a seat, and I'll tell you what he told me."

We plopped down next to a big wheel of Parmesan to hear **THE LEGEND OF THE PHANTOM**.

Now we'll tell you what François told us . . . in our own words, of course!

The Legend of The Phantom

A long, long time ago, before video games or cell phones or even selfies were invented, Monsieur Leroux died, leaving La Première Pâtisserie and his famous recipe book to a very nice man named Jean-Claude.

One day, a not-very-nice man named Jean-Luc stopped by La Première Pâtisserie.

He owned a bakery nearby and offered Jean-Claude a lot of money for a look at Leroux's recipes. Well, that would be like handing your rival team your playbook.

So of course Jean-Claude said, "No, Jean-Luc! No way. Not gonna happen, dude."

Jean-Claude
owner of La Première Pâtisserie
VERY NICE MAN

Jean-Luc
owner of nearby bakery
NOT VERY NICE

BUT the very next day, Jean-Claude was in the bakery and he couldn't find the recipe book any-where. He thought he must have lost it someplace. That was when the Phantom appeared and started going berserk, causing all kinds of chaos in the bakery!

Days went by and the book was still missing, which really bugged you-know-who.

The Phantom got so annoyed, in fact, that he unleashed an army of ghost chefs into the city.

That's right ... chefs who were **GHOSTS!**

One night while Jean-Claude was running from one of those ghost chefs, he just happened to run right by Jean-Luc's bakery.

He spotted a crème brûlée in the window that looked just like Leroux's famous crème brûlée. That was when he realized what had really happened: Jean-Luc had stolen the recipe book!

Jean-Claude confronted Jean-Luc, retrieved the book, and put it back in the bakery. With that, the Phantom disappeared, vowing to return if the recipe book was ever stolen again.

Fin

(That means "The end.")

When François finished telling the story, I looked at my brothers and said, "He vowed to return if the book was ever **STOLEN** again. So Christine didn't lose the book after all. Someone STOLE it. That's why the Phantom is back!"

François started laughing in that belly-shaking, button-bursting way. We were getting really sick of this guy's sense of humor! "You boys are hilarious," he said, even though we had very serious expressions on our faces. "That's just a silly ghost story. The Phantom isn't REAL!"

Turns out "THE PHANTOM ISN'T REAL" isn't something you should say when there's a real phantom around.

Get ready, because this part gets **REALLY GOOD!**

I'M ready!

I didn't mean **YOU**.

The sky outside the shop turned dark, and the lights inside flickered before turning a hair-raising red.

Remember those duck bumps I told you about earlier? They were back and they were all over my body! A laugh echoed through the room, and we turned to François.

"This is no time for laughing, François!" Huey said.

"That wasn't me," he answered.

"Then who was it?" Louie asked.

"IT WAS ME!"

We turned around, and the Phantom was standing directly behind us!

"YOU WANT PROOF THE LEGEND IS TRUE? MEET MY FRIENDS...THEY LOVE FONDUE."

With one snap of his fingers, the Phantom was gone, leaving in his place a horde of horrible, hairy, **HUNGRY** mice! They hurried inside the shop and ran all over the store, chomping on the cheeses.

They crawled over the Camembert, burrowed through the Brie, and built forts in the Roquefort.

My brothers and I aren't usually afraid of mice. Remember, we're pretty much known for our bravery. I'm daring. Huey is heroic.

And though Louie can be leery, even he's not scared of a measly mouse. But these were no ordinary, everyday mice. Their eyes glowed red like the Phantom's mask, and their bodies were translucent (which is just a fancy way of saying "see-through"). These were ghost mice. That's right . . . mice that were **GHOSTS!**

They were chewing through every bit of cheese in the shop. And if that wasn't bad enough, they had started running all over US, too!

They scurried up our arms and darted down our legs. **YUCK!!!** We looked to Cornichon for help, but she was facing off against one particularly monstrous-looking mouse and barking like we'd never heard her bark before.

Meanwhile, François had scrambled onto a tabletop, sending the samples of cheese soaring onto the floor. "They're eating everything! Make them stop!"

"The only one who can stop them is the Phantom," I cried out to him. "Now do you believe he's real?"

"Yes, I believe!" François shouted.

"THE PHANTOM IS REAL!"

And just like that, the ghost mice were gone! The sky outside the shop went back to blue, and the lights inside returned to normal. We looked around, and it was like nothing had happened! The cheese appeared unchewed . . . there wasn't even one noticeable nibble.

But then we saw something behind François. On the blackboard, the list of cheeses was gone and in its place was a message from the Phantom written in red chalk: *OÙ EST LE LIVRE?*

CHAPTER 12

s you can imagine, the mouse attack left SOME of us pretty petrified!

Cornichon was trembling from the top of her furry head to the tip of her fluffy tail. François was sitting beside his table of samples, staring blankly into space. And Louie, who was always the most nervous of the three of us, was pacing back and forth.

He was speechless, which was weird, because, as you may have noticed, Louie **LOVES** to talk!

Huey and I, on the other hand, were handling it like the fearless heroes we are.

Yeah, right! Dewey was shaking in his sneakers, and Huey was hiding behind the big wheel of Parmesan.

Can you blame us?
That was one of the top-ten
most terrifying things
that ever happened to us . . .
well, up until that point, anyway!

But my brothers and I didn't have time to be **TOO** terrified: we had to figure out who stole the recipe book—and fast!

We waved goodbye to freaked-out François, left the funky-smelling *fromagerie*, and ran with Cornichon straight to Christine's house. Sam and Sabine were already there, which was great, because we had **A LOT** to tell them.

We decided to let Louie explain everything that had happened. There was so much to say, and as you may have noticed, Louie **LOVES** to talk.

MET THE OWNER, FRANCOIS!
HEARD THE LEGEND OF THE PHANTOM!!
THE RECIPE BOOK HAD BEEN STOLEN!!!
ATTACKED BY GHOST MICE . . . THAT'S RIGHT,
MICE THAT WERE GHOSTS!!!!

Christine, Sam, and Sabine listened carefully to Louie's every word, and we watched their faces to see how they'd react. It was a real roller coaster of expressions!

First they looked *INTRIGUED*...

then
SHOCKED...

then
SCARED...

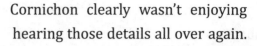

Cornichon clearly wasn't enjoying hearing those details all over again. Around the **SHOCKING** part, she jumped into my lap and licked my face, which made both of us feel a little bit better.

When Louie finally got to the end of the story, he had just enough breath left to say, "So you see, Christine? The book must have been STOLEN!" Then he practically collapsed on the floor.

For a second, Christine looked relieved—probably because she hadn't lost the book after all. But then the truth started sinking in. "Stolen . . . Who would **STEAL** Leroux's recipe book?" she asked.

"That's what we have to figure out!" I said.

"Are these croissants almost ready?" Sam asked eagerly. He and Sabine had gotten distracted and started peering inside the oven, where a dozen of Christine's croissants were turning a yummy golden brown.

We had to stay focused.

"Try to stay focused, you two," I said nicely.

Now, my brothers and I understand how easy it is to get distracted by a nearby snack...

But this was important stuff we were talking about!

Christine agreed. "Yes, AND be patient. Remember, one of the most important parts of baking is pa—"

"Patience. We know," Sabine chimed in. "But how would we even begin to figure out who has the book?" she asked without ever turning away from the oven.

WOW, SABINE MUST REALLY LIKE CHRISTINE'S CROISSANTS, I thought.

"We have to create a list of suspects!" Louie said, keeping the conversation on track.

We asked Christine if she had noticed anyone strange in the bakery the day before the book went missing. She shook her head and said there were just her usual customers. "And I know none of them would steal the book," she added.

Now would be a good time to tell you the first rule of detective work . . .

Never investigate on an empty stomach?

Okay, the **SECOND** rule of detective work . . .

Everyone is a suspect ?

Yep, that's the one!

"There's one thing you have to remember, Christine," I said. "Everyone is a suspect."

Sam turned away from the oven and asked, "What do you mean, 'everyone'?"

Sabine looked in my direction, too. "You mean, like . . . *everyone*?"

I replied to them in my most serious voice. "Yes. Everyone."

For a moment, Christine's kitchen was eerily silent.

It was so quiet we could hear Cornichon's teeth chattering.

DIIIIING!

The timer on the oven DINGED, which broke the silence and scared Cornichon so much she jumped from my lap onto the top of my head, where she held on tight and hid her face in my feathers.

"It's okay, Cornichon," I said, trying to coax her down. She seemed pretty comfortable up there, though, so I let her stay on top of my head while Christine took the croissants out of the oven. She gave us each one, and let me tell you, fresh croissants are without question . . .

THE BEST THING WE'VE EVER TASTED! THE BEST THING WE'VE EVER TASTED! *THE BEST THING WE'VE EVER TASTED!*

That gave me an idea, so I said, "That gives me an idea! Christine, have you ever thought of opening a bakery right here in your house?"

"A bakery right here?" Christine said. "That's not a bad idea!" She smiled at me and giggled at the sight of Cornichon perched on top of my head.

Then, after a moment, she stopped giggling and said, "Sacrebleu!" Remember, that's French for "Oh my goodness!"

"What is it?" I asked.

"Cornichon, you are a genius!" Christine said, scooping Cornichon off my head and spinning her around.

"I just remembered! There WAS a strange customer in the shop the day before the book went missing." She put Cornichon back on top of my head and went on. "Sometimes I would see him pacing back and forth in front of the bakery, though he'd never come inside before. But that day, he did! And he asked me a lot of questions about the croissants, like what's in them, how long I bake them, if there are any secret ingredients. And the strangest thing of all: after asking all those questions, he left without even buying one!"

Just like that, we had a suspect! And we also had a lot of questions . . .

Christine answered our questions one at a time. "I don't know his name. He looked young, tall . . . and kind of cute." She blushed when she said that last thing.

"And Cornichon reminded me of him because of the way she was resting on your head. You see, the man was wearing a very distinctive hat. "It was purple, with a wide brim and a turquoise feather on the side." Just like that, we had a suspect AND a clue!

CHAPTER 13

The next day at school, things started out pretty normal, but when we went to class, we noticed Sam and Sabine weren't at their desks. Later, in the hall, we asked Madame Bouffant if she knew why they weren't in school.

She told us that Monsieur Voland had called to say they didn't feel well and would be staying home all day.

We hoped they would feel better soon, because school wasn't as much fun without them.

PLUS we needed their help tracking down our brand-new suspect. At lunch, we sat at our usual table.

The French word for "table" is "TABLE," but it's pronounced like this: **TAAAA-BLUUUH.**

We each chowed down on our favorite sandwich.

The French word for "sandwich" is "sandwich," and it's pronounced like, well, "sandwich."

While we ate, we talked about the mysterious man in the purple hat.

"We sort of know what he looks like and what kind of hat he wears. So . . . what do we do next?" I asked Huey and Louie.

"Wuuh coooo uuhh mmmmpppnaaa." Louie said something, but we couldn't understand it, because his mouth was full.

"We could ask Monsieur Panache," Huey suggested. Louie swallowed and shouted, "That's what I said!"

"That's not a bad idea, Huey!" I exclaimed. "Monsieur Panache knows *everybody*!"

"Hey, it was myyyy not-bad idea, too!" Louie looked perturbed and took another big bite of his sandwich. **"Wuuh coooo uuhhhh mmmm aaaar olll."**

"We could ask him after school," Huey suggested.

Louie swallowed and shouted even louder, "That's what I said!"

"Great idea, HUEY!" I teased, elbowing Louie in his side.

SEE, LOUIE? THAT WILL TEACH YOU TO TALK WITH YOUR MOUTH FULL.

The rest of the school day was pretty unmemorable except for three things:

1) In history, we had a pop quiz about the Eiffel Tower, which would have been horrible, but we'd learned so much

about the monument from Monsieur Voland that we definitely aced it!

2) One of the other kids brought a drone to show-and-tell.

He showed us how to fly it, and let me tell you . . . it was **AWESOME!**

3) In art, we got to design our very own postcards.

We agreed to send all three of ours to Uncle Donald so we could tell him about everything that had happened in Paris so far: a haywire hot-air balloon ride, a missing recipe book, a menacing Phantom, a mouse attack . . . It would definitely take all three postcards to describe all of that!

After school, we went straight home to Monsieur Panache's apartment to ask if he might know the man in the hat. We squeezed into the tiny slow-moving elevator and inched up to the fifth floor.

When we finally got there, we poured into the hallway and immediately noticed some strange sounds coming from Monsieur Panache's apartment. We pressed our ears up to the door and heard Monsieur Panache shouting things like "No, don't get me! Stay away!" And we could hear Cornichon barking, too.

NO, DON'T GET ME! STAY AWAY!

WOUF, WOUF!

"Do you think the Phantom is in there?" Louie whispered.

"There's only one way to find out!" I said.

"Do we **HAVE** to find out?" Huey asked.

OF COURSE we had to find out! We couldn't leave our awesome host and the world's most awesome dog to fend for themselves against the opposite-of-awesome phantom.

We mustered up all our courage and pulled open the door, and what we saw was truly astounding!

Monsieur Panache was in the living room and he **WAS** shouting, but not at Phantom—at the **TELEVISION**. He was playing one of our video games!

"Hi, boys!" he called out to us cheerfully. "I hope you don't mind. You've been so busy with school and your investigation. I thought I would give one of your video games a try. Is that okay?"

"It's not okay . . ." Huey said, walking over to the sofa, where Monsieur Panache was sitting.

"It's **FANTASTIC!**"

Monsieur Panache looked relieved. "I never knew video games could be this exciting!" he said with a big smile. "Though I don't think I'm very good. I keep getting eaten by a crocodile."

The French word for "crocodile" is "crocodile," but it's pronounced like "croak-oh-dill."

Could you please stop interrupting?

Absolutely!

Thank you.

The French word for "absolutely" is "absolument."

What's the French word for "UGGGGHHHHH"???

Monsieur Panache had picked one of our favorite games: Croc Creek! The goal is to help get a wildlife observer from one side of a croc-infested creek to the other. Sounds easy, right? Well, it is for us, but not for Monsieur Panache.

He hadn't even gotten past the first level.

I decided to make him a deal. "How about this, Monsieur Panache? You take a short break to answer a few questions, and we'll help you beat the game! Sound good?"

"*Oui!*" he answered, putting the controller down on the couch beside him.

"We're looking for a man who was in La Première Pâtisserie a few days ago," Huey explained. "Do you think you could help us figure out who it was?"

"*Oui!*"

"He was young, tall, and, according to Christine, kind of cute." Louis said. "Most importantly, though, he wore a very distinctive hat. It was purple, with a wide brim and—"

"And a turquoise feather on the side!" Monsieur Panache said before Louie could even finish his sentence.

"Yes! Do you know anyone fitting that description?" I asked.

"*Oui, oui!*"

Ha! Monsieur Panache said "wee-wee."

HEY, HUEY?

Yeah, Dewey?

I'M IGNORING YOU FOR THE REST OF THIS CHAPTER.

"That sounds like Pierre Plume." Suddenly, Monsieur Panache had given our suspect a name! We were making such great progress.

"Do you know where we can find him?" I asked.

"*Oui*! He owns a shop called Maison de Chapeaux, which means 'House of Hats.'"

"Okay, last question. And this is really important." Louie's voice got very serious. "Do you think if we go to Maison de Chapeaux, we'll find"—he took a big breath— "a beret that looks good on me?"

Huey and I both rolled our eyes, but Monsieur Panache just laughed. He had been SUCH a big help! Now it was our turn to help him become the master of Croc Creek, so we sat beside him on the sofa.

He picked up the controller, started playing, and immediately got discouraged.

"When I want to go forward, I go backward. When I want to go left . . ."

"You go right?" I asked.

"Yes!" he replied. "How did you know? Let me guess . . . you're a little bit psychic."

I smiled and said, "You're holding the controller upside down."

Once he had the controller the right side up, Monsieur Panache wasn't so bad! He got the wildlife observer from the shore to a raft, dodging a croc to the left and avoiding a croc on the right.

As he played, my brothers and I planned. We knew we had to interrogate Pierre, but how? We could wait until he went back to the bakery. We could "accidentally" bump into him outside his hat shop. We could . . .

"That's a strange-looking croc, isn't it, Cornichon?" Monsieur Panache said in the middle of our brainstorm. "I've never seen a crocodile with a cape before."

"A cape?" I asked.

I had played Croc Creek about a million times, and I'd

never seen a crocodile in a cape, either.

Huey, Louie, and I slowly turned toward the TV, and there, coming out of the creek, was **THE PHANTOM!**

Little by little, he emerged from the water, growing bigger and bigger until he took up the whole screen.

Then he thrust his arms outward, and they came through the front of the television directly toward us. It was like a 3D movie, except we didn't have to wear those funny glasses to see it. It was really

happening right in front of us! Monsieur Panache and Cornichon ran from the living into the kitchen, while my brothers and I took cover behind the couch.

"This guy is really getting on my nerves," Huey whispered.

"That makes two of us," Louie agreed.

"Actually, that makes **THREE** of us!" I added.

We peered over the couch and could see that the top half of the Phantom's body was completely sticking out of the TV. Before long, his whole body would be in the living room! We had to act fast.

"I think this guy has had enough screen time," Huey whispered.

"That makes two of us," Louie agreed.

"Actually, that makes *THREE* of us!" I added.

"And what does Uncle Donald always say when WE'VE had enough screen time?" Huey pointed to an outlet on the wall, where the TV was plugged in. "We've got to *UNPLUG!*"

I'm the daring one, so I offered to do the unplugging while my brothers distracted the Phantom.

"Hey, Phantom," Huey shouted, standing up behind the couch. "I bet your pancakes taste like armpits!"

"Pancakes? Why pancakes??" Louie asked Huey in a hushed voice.

"Breakfast . . . it's the most distracting meal of the day!" Huey exclaimed.

Louie nodded in agreement and called out, "Hey, Phantom! I'll flip you like an omelet!"

The Phantom's pitch-black eyes were fixated on Huey and Louie, giving me enough time to dash to the outlet and grab hold of the cord. Just as the masked madman was about to lunge out of the TV toward my brothers, I held the cord in the air and said the coolest thing ever: *"Au revoir, dude!"* (That means "Goodbye, dude!")

Dewey's right, it was incredibly cool!

Louie's right, it was incredibly, extraordinarily cool!

We all agree for once! If only this moment could last forever . . .

Yeah, that would be tremendous.

Actually, it would be way better than tremendous.
It would be fantastic.

In what world is fantastic way better than tremendous??

Oh, well . . . back to the action!

I pulled the plug from the outlet and watched as the Phantom was sucked back through the screen into the TV until it went completely black.

Just like that, the living room was quiet. Monsieur Panache and Cornichon peeked out from the kitchen to make sure we were safe, and we were. In fact, it was like nothing had happened!

But then we saw it, glowing on the television's dark screen . . . a message from our nemesis in bright red letters:

WANT TO LIVE TO SEE
YOUR NEXT DESSERT?
FIND MY BOOK SOON,
AND NO ONE GETS HURT.

CHAPTER 14

*T*he next day at school, Huey, Louie, and I talked about the best way to investigate Pierre Plume, and we came up with the perfect plan!

WE HAD TO GO . . . PAUSE FOR SUSPENSE . . . UNDERCOVER.

Nicely done, Dewey!

Yeah, you gave me duck bumps . . . the good kind!

We worked out the details during recess. One of us would pretend to be a grown-up and go into Maison de Chapeaux, shopping for a new hat. The only problem was we couldn't agree on which one of us it should be.

Huey thought it should be him because he's so **HAND-SOME** and **HILARIOUS**—his words, not mine. I thought it should be me, because I'm so **DELIGHTFUL** and **DASHING**.

HIS WORDS.
NOT ours.

And Louie thought it should be him, because he's so **LOVABLE** and (for some weird reason) **LOOOVES** berets. We decided there was only one way to choose: Rock Paper Scissors . . .

Huey won, though I'm pretty sure he cheated.

How do you CHEAT at Rock Paper Scissors?
You tell US!

Now that we knew **WHO** would go undercover, we needed to figure out **HOW** to do it. To look like a grown-up, Huey had to be a lot taller. We sat on the playground, talking about how to make that happen, while the other kids took turns flying that awesome drone. Remember the one from show and-tell?

BALLOON

"We could stand on each other's shoulders like we did in the hot-air balloooooooon," I suggested as I slid down the slide.

"Great idea, Dewey!" Louie replied, swinging as high as he could on the swings.

"Orrrrr"—Huey hung upside down on the monkey bars and he pointed at the drone that was hovering near his head—"we could try something a little more high-tech!"

ORRRRR

"Great idea, Huey!" I cheered.

"Yeah, great idea, Huey!" Louie agreed. "So what IS the idea?"

STEP 1: Ask the boy with the drone—his name was Gilbert, by the way—if we could borrow it for the afternoon. We liked Gilbert a lot, because he was nice, he was friendly, and he was about to let us borrow his drone!

STEP 2: Put Huey in one of Monsieur Panache's very long, very grown-up-looking coats. Then sit him on top of the drone and hover it in the air, making him just the right grown-up height.

STEP 3: Fly the Huey-drone combo into the store to distract Pierre, giving us time to look around for the book.

Our perfect plan was going perfectly **UNTIL** STEP 3. This is how things went down . . . literally **DOWN!**

We arrived at the House of Hats, ready to meet our main suspect.

Using the remote, I carefully flew the Huey-topped drone through the front door of the shop, dodging a display to the left and avoiding a hat rack on the right. It wasn't that different from playing Croc Creek . . . and I was GREAT at Croc Creek!

After a few minutes, a man in a wide-brimmed purple hat with a turquoise feather on the side emerged from the back of the shop. It was Pierre! "Hello!" he said to Huey with a big smile. "Can I help you?"

Huey was **SUPPOSED** to keep Pierre busy by asking him a lot of hat-related questions, **BUT** . . .

The drone's propellers were tickling my feet, and all I could do was giggle.

"He he he hello! I'm looking for a new ha ha ha hat!"

"Are you okay, sir?" Pierre looked at Huey with a confused expression.

Meanwhile, Louie quietly snuck into the shop and started looking around.

He was **SUPPOSED** to be searching for Leroux's missing recipe book, **BUT** . . .

There was a big display of beautiful berets, and I ended up looking at those instead.

Outside the shop, I watched through a big glass window. Huey was trying not to laugh, and Louie was just trying on berets.

GET IT TOGETHER, YOU GUYS! THIS IS NOT WHAT WE PLANNED.

I thought.

Then what happened, Dewey?

Yeah, then what happened, Dewey??

Well, I was holding tight to the remote, using all of my video-gaming skills to keep Huey from bumping into anything. I was **SUPPOSED** to keep the drone steady, **BUT** ...

THERE WAS A BEE!

Remember how I feel about bees—the same way I feel about icky cabbages and green goblins and scary phantoms—*I DON'T LIKE THEM!*

I tried to swat the bee away using the only thing I had handy ... the drone remote.

That was a big mistake, because it accidentally sent Huey whizzing around the store.

He sideswiped a shelf of fedoras, plowed into a rack of porkpie hats, and headed straight for Louie.

There was a **BANG,** and a **CRASH,** as Huey and Louie collided and toppled backward into the beret display.

I ran inside the shop, and my brothers were on the floor in a hat-covered heap.

Pierre looked at us, puzzled and perturbed, and started rattling off a bunch of questions. "What's going on here? What's the meaning of this? Is that . . . a DRONE?"

"Hey! We're the ones asking the questions around here," Huey declared, taking off the oversized overcoat.

Now that Huey's cover was blown, we could really begin our interrogation. I started to rattle off some questions of my own: "What were you doing at La Première Pâtisserie a few days ago? Why were you asking so many questions about the croissants? Did you **STEAL** Leroux's famous recipe book?"

Pierre stammered, "*Oui . . .*"

"Aha! So you admit it!" Huey shouted.

"No! I mean, yes I was at La Première Pâtisserie. And I was asking a lot of questions be- cause . . . because . . ."

"Because what?" Louie asked forcefully.

"Because I have a crush on Christine LeBlanc!"

As Pierre blurted it out, his cheeks turned as red as Huey's sweatshirt. "I've gone by her bakery so many times, and the other day, I finally worked up the courage to go in. I even wore my best hat. But once I saw her, I got so flustered that all I could talk about was croissants. I was so nervous I forgot to even buy one!"

"So you don't know anything about Leroux's famous recipe book?" I asked.

"Whose famous what now?" Pierre looked genuinely confused.

"Hey, you guys," Louie said quietly, "I think he's telling the truth."

LOUIE IS BASICALLY A HUMAN LIE-DETECTOR TEST.

It's true! I can always tell if someone is lying or telling the truth.

I can, too!

That's not true . . .

Louie believed Pierre, and to be honest, so did I. After all, he'd come right out and told us about his crush on Christine, and it's not easy to admit when you like someone.

JUST LOOK AT HUEY! HE STILL WON'T ADMIT THAT HE HAD A CRUSH ON SOPHIE KELLER BACK IN BERLIN.

Because I didn't!

CHAPTER
15

By the time we helped
Pierre clean up the mess
and apologized for making
the mess in the first place, it
was starting to get late.

We knew Monsieur Pa-
nache and Cornichon would
have dinner waiting for us,
so we decided to head home. It wouldn't take long;
it was only about a fifteen minute walk from the House
of Hats to the house of our hosts.

But it would feel like one of the longest walks *EVER!*

Allow me to set the scene: They call Paris
the City of Lights, but that night, it seemed much
DARKER than usual. They also call Paris the City
of Love, but that night, there was a chill in the air
that I didn't *LOVE* at all.

As we passed by the Panthéon—that cool building
Sam and Sabine told us about—we started hearing a

strange, unsettling sound behind us. At first, I thought it was Huey's stomach growling.

"Geez, Huey! You must be *really* hungry," I teased him.

"Well, it is dinnertime, and I am *really* hungry," he said. "But that wasn't me!"

"He's telling the truth," Louie, the human lie-detector test, confirmed.

As we walked by the university, there wasn't a student in sight. *How weird*, I was thinking when I heard the sound again. It was a disturbing mix of growling and snarling and drooling . . . and it was getting closer!

"See! I told you that wasn't me," Huey said proudly.

"Then . . . what was it?" Louie asked.

"There's only one way to find out." I gathered up all my courage and turned around to see what was making the noise. There, in the light of the full moon, was the silhouette of a dog.

But this was no sweet, snuggly, super-cute Cornichon kind of dog. This was a ginormous, monstrous, super-colossal dog, like the creature from my nightmare! In fact, this was no DOG at all . . . it was a we—

WAIT! I've been looking forward to this moment the entire book. Can I please say it? Pleeeease?

OKAY, FINE!

It was A WEREWOLF!!!

There was only one thing to do . . . RUUUUUNNNNN!!!

Huey, Louie, and I bolted from one street to the next, running faster than we'd ever run before. Our feet moved at **TURBO SPEED**, but somehow that **THING** was still gaining on us. As we sprinted along the Seine River, we could hear it panting and howling. It was hot on our tails!

Finally, we turned onto Monsieur Panache's street and darted through the front door of the building. There was no time to take the tiny, slow-moving elevator, so we raced up the stairs all the way to the fifth floor.

Once inside the apartment, we ran over to the living room's large windows and looked down, but there was no sign of the werewolf.

We were safe! Or were we?

"Do you think the Phantom is responsible for this?" Huey asked in a hushed voice.

"Maybe!" I replied, peeking out the window.

"Do you think the werewolf will come back?" Louie asked nervously.

But before I could answer, I heard something creeping up behind us . . . It was panting and licking its lips.

Then it let out a loud sound:

"WOUF, WOUF!"

"AHHHHHHHHHHH!!!"

We screamed so loudly they probably heard us all the way back in Duckburg! But then we realized it wasn't the ginormous, monstrous, super-colossal werewolf. It was just sweet, snuggly, super-cute Cornichon. And she was the only dog we wanted to see for a while.

CHAPTER 16

A Phantom, ghost mice, and an actual, real, live werewolf...

Now you can see why we call Paris the City of FRIGHTS!

AND THE FRIGHTS WEREN'T OVER YET...

Even though we were totally freaked out by **the werewolf,** we still went to school the next day. After all, we were part of the National Association of **STUDIOUS** and Talented Youth! Luckily, Sam and Sabine were back in class.

At lunch, we all sat at our usual table, eating our favorite sandwiches and looking pretty *misérable.* (That's French for "miserable.")

We looked that way for a few reasons:

1) There was a masked madman out to get us.

2) We had a werewolf on our tails.

3) Gilbert would never trust us with his drone again.

And to top it off, our list of suspects had gone from one to **NONE**.

We were finishing our sandwiches—and sulking—when Madame Bouffant bounced over to our table. "You look like you could use some good news!" she said cheerfully, handing each one of us a very fancy-looking envelope. The back of mine said *DEWEY DUCK* in swirly royal-blue letters.

I tore it open, and inside, there was an invitation!

"What does 'part deux' mean?" Louie asked Sam and Sabine.

"Part Two," they replied.

"Whoa, she's actually doing it," I said excitedly. "Christine is opening a bakery in her house!"

"NICE!" Huey started licking his lips and rubbing his stomach. "I'm going to eat at least twenty croissants!"

YOU ARE INVITED TO THE GRAND OPENING OF LA PREMIÈRE PÂTISSERIE
PART DEUX
WHERE: CHRISTINE LEBLANC'S CHATEAU
WHEN: TODAY AT 3 PM

"But what about the Phantom?" Louie, who was always the most anxious of the three of us, was pacing back and forth beside the lunch table.

"Great job, Louie!" Huey said sarcastically. "Thanks to you, I've lost my appetite. Now I'll probably only eat nineteen croissants . . . "

Louie was too worried about the Phantom to worry about Huey's appetite. He turned to me and asked, "Do you think he'll show up, Dewey?"

"There's only one way to find out," I told him.

That afternoon, the five of us went to Christine's house for the grand opening, and we weren't the only ones.

It seemed like most of Paris was there!

There were people—and delicious-looking goodies—all over the place.

First we spotted François telling jokes by a table covered in tarts. Then we saw Pierre wearing his favorite hat and standing quietly by a punch bowl.

Even Madame Bouffant was there, chatting cheerfully with a bunch kids from school.

At the center of the room was a display of macarons in the shape of the Eiffel Tower.

It looked **YUMMY, DELICIOUS, AND BEAUTIFUL-YUMALICIOUSFUL!**

While admiring the mouthwatering tower, we noticed Monsieur Panache and Cornichon across the room. We walked over to them to say hello, and right away Cornichon started acting funny. She sniffed Sam, let out a **WOUF**, and then turned her nose to his sister.

We didn't know why, but she began tugging at Sabine's backpack with her teeth.

"Leave Sabine's backpack alone, Cornichon," Monsieur Panache said.

"That's okay, Monsieur Panache! She must smell the cookies I had in there earlier," Sabine replied with an uneasy giggle.

"Here you go, girl!" She grabbed a mad-eleine off a nearby table and handed it to Cornichon, who immediately plopped down on the floor to enjoy the treat.

"Wait a second . . ." Louie, the human lie-detector test, looked at Sabine with a leery expression.

Louie always looks leery, but this time, he looked even leerier usual. "I don't think that's true . . ." he said, but before he could finish his thought, Christine bounded into the room, carrying a tray of piping hot croissants. She put them down on a table and got the attention of the guests.

"I'd like to thank you all for coming today!" she said happily. "I'd especially like to thank DEWEY DUCK, who had the great idea to open a bakery right here in my house!"

My cheeks turned as red as the punch Pierre was drinking.

"Due to some, well, very un-expected events, I didn't have any recipes to use. So I baked these all from memory. I hope you enjoy them. Bon appétit!"

The crowd cheered, and the clapping and whooping were so loud we could hardly hear the menacing laugh echoing through the room. But soon that creepy cackle grew so loud that everyone—even François—got quiet.

Then the sky outside the house turned dark.

I'm having Deja BOO again!

Me BOO! I mean, me TOO!

Suddenly, the front door slammed open, and standing there was the MOST uninvited guest . . . **THE PHANTOM**. His cape whipped in the wind behind him, and his black eyes glared out through his red mask.

We've already established that his outfit was extremely freaky. And get THIS: he had added another sinister accessory—a cane. He slammed it down on the ground and spoke . . . and boy, did he have a lot to say!

"YES, THANK YOU FOR COMING, AND BON APPÉTIT! WHAT I HAVE IN STORE WILL BE OH SO SWEET. I SEE YOU BROUGHT YOUR APPETITES. PLEASE ALLOW ME TO PROVIDE THE FRIGHTS!"

With that, the Phantom snapped his fingers, and hundreds of the horrible, hairy ghost mice appeared.

"NOT AGAIN!" François screamed, jumping onto the tart-covered table. It was just like in the *fromagerie*! The red-eyed rodents crawled all over the croissants, bathed in the crème brûlée, and tunneled through every éclair. They even destroyed t he display of macarons!

And not only that, but they scurried up the legs and down the shirts of all the people in the bakery while nibbling at every stray crumb. They even burrowed inside Madame Bouffant's hair!

"WHAT A WONDERFUL PARTY. IT'S TRULY DELICIOUS!
NOW IT'S TIME WE MIXED IN SOMETHING MALICIOUS.
A PINCH OF TERROR, A SPRINKLE OF WOE,
AND A COUPLE MORE GHOSTS . . . JUST A DOZEN OR SO!"

Then the Phantom snapped his fingers again, and twelve ghost chefs instantly appeared in the room.

That's right . . . chefs who were **GHOSTS!** Just like the ghost-mice, their eyes glowed red, and their bodies were translucent. (Remember, that's a fancy word for "see-through.") They wore black aprons that matched their black chefs' hats, and they each carried an evil-looking kitchen tool: there were sifters and graters and rolling pins!

The grand opening was quickly becoming a great big disaster! Crepes and custards and croissants were flying through the air. Ghost mice and ghost chefs and non-ghost people were clamoring all over the place.

We watched as one of the ghost chefs pushed Pierre's head—favorite hat and all—into the punch bowl. Christine ran over to help him, but another ghost chef started chasing her around the kitchen with a whisk for a weapon.

And all the while, the Phantom stood perfectly still in the doorway, watching over the chaos proudly.

Then he said:

"YOU DIDN'T DO WHAT YOU WERE TOLD, AND REVENGE IS A CROISSANT BEST SERVED COLD."

He whipped his cape around his body and instantly went from the doorway to the middle of the room.

That's called teleportation!
It's the ability to move from one place to another without crossing the space between.

Telekinesis, teleportation . . . this guy could do everything!

EXCEPT TALK WITHOUT RHYMING!

"SOMEONE STOLE MY BOOK,
AND UNTIL I KNOW WHO,
I'LL STEAL SOMETHING
OF YOURS . . .
COMPRENEZ VOUS?"

"What does 'comprenez vous' mean?" Louie asked Sam and Sabine. "'Do you understand?'" they replied. "No, that's why I asked!"

"YOU DON'T UNDERSTAND? THEN JUST WAIT AND SEE. COME ON, LITTLE DOG. YOU'RE COMING WITH ME."

That's when the nasty, lousy, rotten phantom did the nastiest, lousiest, rottenest thing *YET!*

He grabbed Cornichon from the floor, whipped his cape around his body, and made them both disappear . . .

CHAPTER 17

"WOUF, WOUF, WOUF, WOUF, WOUF!"

We could hear Cornichon barking, and it sounded like it was coming from outside the house. As we ran to the front lawn, Sam and Sabine must have gotten lost in all the chaos, because when my brothers and I got there, they were nowhere to be found.

Above our heads, a bolt of lightning cracked and filled the sky with a bright white light. "*THERE HE IS!*" Huey shouted, pointing to the very top of the house.

We looked up—WAY up—and saw the scary silhouette of the Phantom standing on Christine's roof. He stared down at us on the sidewalk, thrust his cane into the air, and let out a creepy laugh that made all the feathers on the back of my neck stand up. We were way past duck bumps!

"**AND THERE HE GOES!**" Huey yelled. The Phantom tucked Cornichon inside his cape and leaped from the top of the house to the roof of the building next door. Then he jumped to the next roof and the next, as easily as if he was jumping over a puddle.

"COME ON, GUYS!" I shouted. "HE'S GETTING AWAY." We couldn't let him escape with Cornichon, so we all took off running in the direction that masked troublemaker was heading. At least, I thought we all took off running, but Louie didn't budge.

Okay, okay! They already heard all of this in the prologue. Just go over the HIGHLIGHTS so we can get to the next part!

You just don't want Dewey to remind everyone that you were too scared to chase after the Phantom.

That's not true! And I would know. I'm a human lie-detector test, remember?

YOU MAKE A GOOD POINT, LOUIE! WE COVERED ALL OF THIS IN THE PROLOGUE. SO HERE ARE THE HIGHLIGHTS.

Even though Louie didn't want to at first, all three of us followed the Phantom to the center of the city and watched as he used his cane to pole-vault from the edge of a building onto the side of the Eiffel Tower. Once there, he climbed all the way to the top and let out the wildest laugh yet.

Guess how many steps it is to the top of the Eiffel Tower.

It's 1,665 steps!

I didn't mean **YOU**.

But it **IS** 1,665 steps!

AND WE WERE ABOUT TO CLIMB UP EACH AND EVERY ONE!

We raced to the top of the Eiffel Tower, which was equal parts exciting AND exhausting! And when we got there, we didn't even have time to catch our breath, because we immediately came face to face with the Phantom. He was holding Cornichon, who trembled from head to tail.

Louie looked at our favorite pup in the arms of our least favorite person and **LOST IT!** "Give us back our dog, you wicked old phantom!" he shouted, which was very un-Louie-like.

But that didn't seem to bother the Phantom at all. He tucked Cornichon back inside his cape and said:

"I'VE BEEN PATIENT AND I'VE BEEN FAIR,
BUT TIME'S ALMOST UP, SO YOU'D BETTER BEWARE.
FIND MY BOOK BY THE END OF THE DAY,
OR I'LL COOK UP A CORNICHON SOUFFLE."

Then he did that teleportation thing again!

He snapped his fingers and disappeared, leaving three red-eyed ghost chefs in his place.

They each had an eggbeater in one hand. Now, an eggbeater may not sound very scary, but when those shiny metal beaters are turned up to top speed and coming right toward you, they are *TERRIFYING!*

And the worst part was the ghost chefs stood between us and the stairs.

THERE WAS NO WAY DOWN!

We didn't know what to do. For the first time **EVER**, we were completely out of ideas. We didn't even have any **BAD** ideas!

With their eggbeaters whirling furiously, the ghost chefs slowly inched closer to us until our backs were against the side of the tower. There was nowhere left to go . . .

IT WAS ALL OVER FOR US!

Finished.

FINITO.

FIN. REMEMBER THAT MEANS "THE END."

CHAPTER 18

JUST KIDDING!

That's not actually THE END!

We still have, like, four more chapters!

AND THINGS ARE ABOUT TO GET EVEN MORE EXCITING!

The ghost chefs had pushed us all the way to the edge of the tower. WE'RE TOTAL GONERS, I thought BETTER SAY GOODBYE TO MY BROTHERS.

"Goodbye, Huey. Goodbye, Louie."

They both turned to me and said, "Goodbye, De—"

"DEEEWWWEEEY!" Suddenly, two voices were shouting my name, and I recognized them immediately: it was Sam and Sabine!

Huey, Louie, and I turned around to see our friends flying beside the Eiffel Tower in their father's hot-air balloon. They positioned the basket directly beside the platform and yelled, "JUMP IN!"

Without even thinking (or looking down), we dove from the tower into the hot-air balloon. Right that second, the ghost chefs lunged forward to grab us, but we were already out of reach.

Once we were safe in the basket, we had a lot of questions for Sam and Sabine.

What are you doing here?

Where did you come from?

HOW ARE YOU ABLE TO FLY THIS BALLOON? ISN'T THE BURNER TOO HIGH TO REACH?

"We saw you chasing the Phantom toward the Eiffel Tower and we thought you might need some backup," Sam explained. "So we ran to the park to pick up the balloon!"

"After our last flight, we worked with our dad to make the burner's nozzle low enough for a twelve-year-old kid to reach," Sabine told us. "You know, in case of bad weather."

My brothers and I gave Sam and Sabine a supertight, "thank you for saving us" squeeze.

This time, THEY were the HEROES!

"So it's five heroes against one phantom!" I said, putting my hands firmly on my hips.

"Yeah, let's confront this guy once and for all!" Huey exclaimed.

"And most importantly, get Cornichon back!" Louie hollered. "To the bakery!"

Sam and Sabine sailed the hot-air balloon toward La Première Pâtisserie (part one) and landed right in front of the royal blue awning. We peeked inside, but there was no sign of the phantom—only the glass case full of once delicious-looking treats that were looking not so delicious.

"I have an idea," Sam said in a hushed voice. "We can go around the back to the open kitchen window."

The five of us snuck around to the other side of the bakery, and when we got there, we couldn't believe our eyes. In the center of the room, Cornichon was trapped in a dog cage made entirely of gingerbread.

She was trying to eat her way through, but as soon as she'd finish one piece, another would appear in its place. "We've got to get her out of there," I whispered to the others. "Come on!"

One by one, we squeezed through the open crack in the window. We were being as quiet as mice—regular mice, not ghost mice—but when Cornichon saw us, she was so happy that she let out a *"WOUF, WOUF, WOUF!"*

We tried to shush her, but she couldn't help herself. Her tail was wagging harder than we'd ever seen it wag before!

"WOUF, WOUF, WOUF, WOUF, WOUF, WOUF, WOUF, WOUF!"

Then the pantry door slammed open, and Cornichon stopped barking. A cloud of sugar, salt, and flour burst into the kitchen, and in the very center of it was the Phantom.

He stepped forward to speak AND for the first time he didn't rhyme!

"Are you ready to tell me who has my book?" he asked in a weirdly gentle voice, which was somehow even creepier than his normal angry voice.

"We don't know!" Huey replied.

"But it's definitely not us!" I said forcefully.

"You've got the wrong kids. *Comprenez vous*?" Louie squeaked out, using all the bravery he could muster.

"Yeah, it's not us!" Sam stomped his foot.

"We don't have it!" Sabine stomped her foot, too.

"Wait a second…" Louie, the human lie-detector test, got that very leery look again.

"There's something fishy going on here…"

But before Louie could explain, the Phantom began moving his arms around in a circle, whipping up the biggest cloud of sugar, salt, and flour yet. And in the very center of it, a creature appeared.

It was a ten-foot-tall monster made entirely of an ooey-gooey, creepy-creamy substance. "Whoa . . ." Sam said in astonishment. "It's a CRÈME BRÛLÉE BEAST!"

You'd think a monster made of rich, sugary custard would be sweet.

But this thing was ANYTHING but sweet!

As the cloud around it vanished, the monster raised up its arms, sending bits of crème brûlée flying across the room. It began to lumber toward us, destroying everything in its path—including the gingerbread cage!

Once Cornichon was free, we all ran together to take cover inside the pantry. Sam slammed the door behind us. "It can't get in here, *RIGHT*?" he asked.

But he was *WRONG*. Oh, so very wrong!

It turns out a monster made entirely of crème brûlée can liquefy, turning itself into a puddle that can easily slither under the door. I watched in horror as that ooey-gooey, creepy-creamy substance oozed into the pantry.

We tried using anything we could find to block the gap—towels . . . aprons . . . Huey even sacrificed his most favorite sweatshirt—but nothing could keep it out!

Cornichon tried to lap it up with her tongue, but as soon as she'd finish licking some, more would appear in its place.

"It's bound to get in!" Louie screamed.

"Let it," Sabine said in a strangely calm voice as she quickly searched the pantry shelves. "Sam, crème brûlée calls for a DASH of cinnamon, but add too much and . . ."

Sam thought for a second before saying, "And you'll ruin it!"

"Exactly!" Sabine grabbed a large jar of cinnamon off the shelf and held it out to us so we could each take a big handful. We stood back and let the slimy substance flow into the pantry.

"Throw the cinnamon on the count of three!" Sabine told us.

Every last drop crept under the door until the crème brûlée creep was entirely inside the pantry. Then it rematerialized right in front of our eyes, going from flat puddle to ten-foot-tall terror in a matter of seconds. Our jaws dropped as the beast opened its icky-sticky mouth and let out a roar so loud it shook every jar on every shelf.

"READY?" Sabine shouted over the deafening sound. "*Un, deux, TROIS!*"

On the count of three, we each threw a handful of cinnamon at the creature, which sent it flying backward through the pantry door.

It started twisting and shaking and sending bits of crème brûlée soaring all over the kitchen. The plan was working! The cinnamon was mixing with the ooey-gooey, creepy-creamy substance, and the more the monster moved, the more the spice mixed in.

Finally, the beast opened its mouth to let out one last **ROAR** before turning into a sloppy cinnamon-filled mess right at the Phantom's feet.

CHAPTER 19

"YOU RUINED MY RENOWNED CRÈME BRÛLÉE!"

The Phantom cried out in dismay as he leaned over the defeated—and totally disgusting—creature.

Then he stood up straight and stared at us with an eerily calm expression.

We expected him to be FURIOUS . . . but he wasn't! Weird, huh??

That guy could really keep us on our webbed toes. He was FULL of surprises!

AND WHAT HE DID NEXT WAS THE MOST SURPRISING THING OF ALL . . . HE TOOK OFF HIS MASK!

We watched as the Phantom removed the creepy red disguise, showing us his face for the first time.

He looked **JUST** like Monsieur Leroux, whose portrait was still hanging on the wall next to the rack of rolling pins.

MONSIEUR LEROUX LOOKALIKE

MONSIEUR LEROUX

"Whoa, you look **A LOT** like Monsieur Leroux!" Huey said in amazement.

"That's because **I AM** . . . or **I WAS**," he told us while straightening the painting ever so slightly.

"Christine said a phantom is the spirit of someone from long ago," Louie squeaked out nervously. "So that means you're a . . . a . . ."

"A ghost." Louie was too freaked out to finish his sentence, so the Phantom finished it for him.

"This bakery used to belong to me, and all of these recipes are mine. By the way, my famous crème brûlée only calls for a **DASH** of cinnamon," he added, shaking his head. "We know," Sabine said haughtily, giving Sam a sly low five.

"But if we had followed **YOUR RECIPE**, we would have been **TOAST!**" Sam added as he slapped her hand proudly.

When Sam said that, I could practically see the light bulbs go off above my brothers' heads, and I'm sure they could see the one going off above mine.

Definitely!

Absolutely!

IN FACT, EVEN CORNICHON COULD SEE IT!

WOUF, WOUF!

Suddenly, it was as clear as the water of the long river that ran across the city . . . we knew who had stolen the recipe book!

Remember the SECOND rule of detective work:

Everyone is a suspect. EVERYONE.

EVEN OUR BEST FRIENDS!

"Wait a second . . ." Louie said, turning toward Sam and Sabine.

"The very first time we went to the bakery, Christine told you that you weren't ready to learn the recipe for crème brûlée yet," Huey continued.

"The only way you could have known how to defeat the monster is if . . ."

As I said that, Sam and Sabine went from looking proud and haughty to looking meek and caught-y. With her head down, Sabine unzipped the large compartment of her backpack—the one Cornichon had been tugging at earlier. She reached inside and pulled out LEROUX'S FAMOUS RECIPE BOOK!

"**WOUF, WOUF, WOUF, WOUF!**" Cornichon barked at the sight of the book.

"You and your nose were right, girl," Sabine said, stroking Cornichon's fluffy white head. "The book was in here all along. I shouldn't have distracted you with a madeleine."

Now that we knew **WHO** had stolen the book, we wanted to know **WHY** they would do it.

"We dream of becoming bakers as talented as Christine, but it's just taking so long," Sabine explained, hugging the book against her chest.

"And we've never been very patient. So we thought we could borrow the book and practice some of the recipes before anyone even noticed it was gone. We never meant to **STEAL IT**."

Now that we knew **WHO** had stolen the book and **WHY** they had done it, we wanted to know **HOW**.

"It happened the day of the haywire hot-air balloon ride, when we brought you here for the first time and had that yummy *pain au chocolat*," Sam told us. "We waited until Christine locked up before sneaking in through the open kitchen window and borrowing the book."

"We had always planned to return it, but the very next day, you-know-who was already here," Sabine said, motioning her head toward of the Phantom, who was listening to their confession contentedly.

"We even pretended to be sick one day and took off from school so we could come to the bakery when no one was around. We were going to put it back . . . but we chickened out," Sam said, dropping his head against his chest.

WE'RE SO, SO SORRY!

For once, Huey, Louie, and I were speechless. But that didn't matter, because the Phantom had plenty to say.

"FINALLY A CONFESSION! WHAT A SHAME IT'S TOO LATE. YOU THINK YOU'RE SORRY NOW . . . WELL, JUST YOU WAIT."

The Phantom had started rhyming again . . .
a very bad sign!

He snapped his fingers and a dozen of those ghastly ghost chefs appeared in the kitchen.

Then he said something to them in French that

my brothers and I couldn't understand: *"Récupérer mon livre, s'il vous plait."*

"*Livre* . . . that means 'book'!" Huey hollered. "Sabine, look out!"

The ghost chefs raised their whisks and eggbeaters above their heads and began moving swiftly toward Sabine, who was still holding tight to the book.

"Hey, Sabine!" I shouted as the ghost chefs got closer to her. "How about a game of keep-away?"

"That's not a bad idea," she said.

Sabine tossed me the book, and all the ghost chefs turned their heads in my direction.

They started coming my way, so I tossed the book to Sam, who tossed it to Huey, who tossed it to Louie, who dropped it in a big bowl of old dough.

Catching is not my strong suit!

Neither is throwing. Or kicking. Or dribbling. Or bowling . . . You're particularly bad at bowling . . .

Okay, they get it!

We all watched as the book sank to the bottom of the bowl. Right away, Louie pushed up the sleeves of

his shirt and started digging. He was up to his elbows in dough, and the ghost chefs were headed right toward him.

That is, until Cornichon intervened!

"WOUF, WOUF, WOUF, WOUF!" she woofed, but these weren't her typical friendly or excited WOUFS.

They were angry WOUFS. She grabbed hold of a ghost chef's black apron, pulling the menacing mischief-maker backward away from my brother.

"I got it!" Louie shouted as he pulled his arms out of the bowl, holding the book in his right hand. He shook off the dough, ran to the shelf beneath Monsieur Leroux's portrait, and returned the recipes to their rightful place.

And single–handedly saved the day!

UM . . . excuse me?

IT TOOK ALL OF OUR HANDS TO SAVE THE DAY!

Fine . . . And six-handedly saved the day!

In an instant, all of the ghost chefs turned into clouds of sugar, salt, and flour that sprinkled softly onto the floor. We could feel them crunching under our feet as we ran to the center of the kitchen and huddled together, waiting to see what the ghost of Monsieur Leroux would do next.

He looked at the book, safe on the shelf, turned to us, and said, "*Merci beaucoup!*" (That's French for "thank you very much.")

That's when he did the most **SHOCKING** thing yet—even more shocking than removing his mask. He smiled!

"My recipe book is back where it belongs. And that's where it will stay," he told us. "If it doesn't, I'll be back. *Comprenez vous?*"

Then, in one swift motion, he whipped his cape around his body and disappeared.

He must have done that teleportation thing again, but we didn't know where he was going.

And we didn't care. He was GONE!

OR SO WE THOUGHT . . .

CHAPTER 20

*T*he five of us stood together in the center of the kitchen and no one said a word. We were still speechless! Then we heard noises coming from the front of the bakery.

"Oh no! Not more ghost chefs!" Huey pleaded.

"Or more ghost mice!" Louie cried.

"Or ghosts of any kind!" I shouted as the door of the kitchen started to swing open.

We held our breath and closed our eyes, waiting for whatever creepy thing would appear next.

But there were no ghost chefs. No ghost mice. No ghosts of any kind! When the door finally swung open, we saw that it was Christine walking into the kitchen, with Monsieur Panache behind her.

"Kids! We've been looking all over for you!" Christine exclaimed.

"Thank goodness you're all right!" Monsieur Panache called out. He scooped us all up, including Cornichon. "I was so worried about you!"

As we hugged our awesome host, Sam and Sabine ran and jumped into Christine's open arms. "What happened?" she asked them.

Even though it wasn't easy, Sam and Sabine confessed everything to Christine, who listened quietly. Once they had explained the **WHO, WHAT, WHEN, WHERE,** and **HOW,** they both apologized again: "**WE'RE SO, SO SORRY!**"

After a moment, Christine let out a small sigh. "*Ah, mes amies . . .* you are sweet, kind, and hardworking, but you are not patient. I promise to teach you every recipe if you promise never again to take anything from the bakery without asking."

"We promise!" Sam assured her.

"AND if you promise to help me clean up this mess," Christine added, looking around the chaotic, crème brûlée–covered room. Every single thing was out of place—except, of course, the recipe book.

And above it, hanging perfectly straight, was the portrait of Monsieur Leroux.

"We promise!" Sabine said.

Christine gave Sam and Sabine another reassuring squeeze and smiled. "So you mastered crème brûlée all on your own?"

"*Oui,*" Sabine replied. "But I don't think we'll make it again for a long, long time."

EPILOGUE

It took a few weeks to get the bakery back to **how it was before the Phantom** turned everything topsy-turvy, but we all pitched in! Huey, Louie, and I went every day after school to clean up. Cornichon came, too, and sniffed out leftover bits of sugar, salt, and flour (and licked them off the floor).

Even Pierre lent a hand! Turns out once you come face to face with a ghost chef, talking to your crush seems a lot less scary.

But no one helped out more than Sam and Sabine.

They went to the bakery before and after school and even during **RECESS**.

One day at lunch, we were all sitting at our usual table, eating our favorite sandwiches, when Madame Bouffant bounced over to us.

There was something different about her. Turns out once your hairdo is home to a ghost mouse, changing your style seems like a good idea. "You must be making great progress at the bakery!" she said cheerfully, handing each one of us a very fancy-looking envelope.

Inside was another invitation!

YOU ARE INVITED TO
THE GRAND OPENING OF
LA PREMIÈRE PÂTISSERIE
PART TROIS

WHERE: LA PREMIERE PATISSERIE
WHEN: TODAY AT 3PM

"NICE!" Huey started licking his lips and rubbing his stomach. "I'm going to eat at least thirty croissants!" And this time, there was no phantom to ruin his appetite.

That afternoon, the five of us went to the grand opening, and it was a great, big success!

Once again, the glass case that ran from one end of the bakery to the other was filled with rows and rows of every kind of yummy thing you could imagine.

I won't describe them to you because I don't want to start drooling again . . . but I will SHOW them to you!

During the party, Huey and Louie stood with Monsieur Panache and Cornichon at the center of the bakery, enjoying cups of creamy chocolate mousse.

Meanwhile, I was pressing my beak against the case, trying to get a closer look at what seemed like a mash-up of a tart and a croissant—a troissart—when all of a sudden a face appeared on the other side of the glass.

"Boo!" the face said. But this time, I didn't jump. It was just Christine! She smiled, came out from behind the counter, and got everyone's attention.

"I'd like to thank you all for coming today!" she said happily. "I'd especially like to thank my junior apprentices, SAM AND

SABINE VOLAND. They helped me bake all of these delicious treats."

Everyone cheered for Sam and Sabine, who gave each other a sly low five. And we cheered the loudest of all! Because even though they were the culprits, they were still our friends.

Then Christine turned to the three of us. "And I'd like to give the biggest thanks of all to HUEY, DEWEY, and LOUIE DUCK. None of this would have been possible without them. Soon they'll be off saving the day in a new country, and we'll miss them terribly. But for now, please join me in saying 'Hooray for the international student HEROES!'"

We gave Christine a big hug as the whole crowd shouted, "*HOORAY!*"

And in that moment, we felt a lot of things:

Proud to have solved the mystery and stopped the Phantom!

Sad to be leaving Paris and all the cool people we met there!

EXCITED TO BE HEADING OFF TO OUR NEXT DESTINATION!

And in the middle of all those feelings was another emotion that's hard to describe: it was a mix of curiosity and creeped-out-ness. Because even though we'd gotten rid of the Phantom, one mystery was still unsolved.

I turned to Huey and Louie and asked, "Where do you think that *WEREWOLF* came from?"

Huey shrugged and said, "Beats me!"

Louie scratched his head, adding, "No clue!"

And he was right. We didn't have a single clue. We didn't know *WHERE* it came from or *WHO* sent it or *HOW* it found us all the way in Paris.

"I guess we may never find out!" I said.

"WOUF, WOUF!"

"Hi, Cornichon!" We'd been so busy talking about the werewolf, we hadn't even noticed that our fluffy white friend was staring up at us with her perfectly round face. We were really going to miss Cornichon when it was time to leave Paris.

And Huey would have to keep much better track of his hat in the next city!

I leaned down to pet her and saw that she'd dropped something at our feet. "What is that, girl?" I asked and bent down to pick it up.

"Oh, that came for you earlier today!" Monsieur Panache said. We were going to miss Monsieur Panache a ton, too! We smiled at him, but he must have noticed a sort of sad look on our faces, because he gave us a big best-host-ever hug before heading over to a display of macarons in the shape of the Arc de Triomphe.

"It's a postcard," I told my brothers, shaking off some of Cornichon's slobber.

"It must be from Uncle Donald!" Huey exclaimed.

"He probably got our postcards, and now he's writing back!" Louie said cheerfully.

So much had happened over the last few weeks, I had completely forgotten about the postcards we'd made in art class and mailed home to Uncle Donald.

"Awesome!" I said.

But when I turned the postcard over, it was anything but awesome— it was *HORRIBLE*. (That's French for "HORRIBLE.")

DR. Z?!?!?!

NOT AGAIN!

GOSH, WHAT'D WE DO TO MAKE THAT MAD SCIENTIST SO . . . SO . . . MAD???

BONJOUR, YOU NOSY LITTLE YOUNGSTERS! I HOPE YOU ENJOYED THE SURPRISE I UNLEASHED ON YOU IN PARIS. A WEREWOLF MAKES SUCH A DELIGHTFULLY TERRIFYING PET, DON'T YOU THINK? AND IF YOU THOUGHT THAT WAS A SCREAM, WAIT UNTIL YOU SEE WHAT I HAVE PLANNED FOR YOU AT YOUR NEXT STOP!

SINCERELY, DR. Z

My brothers and I looked at the postcard in disbelief. Then we looked at each other with eyes as wide as macarons.

"Hey, guys," Louie said, "how do you say 'uh-oh' in French?"

— FIN —

REMEMBER, THAT MEANS "THE END."

Suzanne Sheridan

ABOUT THE AUTHOR

Tommy Greenwald's *Game Change*r is on fourteen state lists, was an Amazon Best Book of the Month, a YALSA Top Ten pick, and a Junior Library Guild Premier selection. Greenwald is also the author of the Crimebiters! and Charlie Joe Jackson series, among many other books for children. Day job–wise, Tommy is the cofounder of Spotco Advertising, a theatrical and entertainment advertising agency in New York City, and the lyricist and co-bookwriter (with Andrew Lippa) of *John & Jen*, an off-Broadway musical that has been produced around the country and internationally. To read woefully outdated information about him, visit tommygreenwald.com.

ABOUT THE ILLUSTRATOR

Elisa Ferrari was born in Verona, Italy, in 1988. She is a self-taught artist. After graduating from university, she started working as an art assistant and then as a complete comic artist and illustrator for different magazines and publishing houses. In Italy she served as an artist for publishing houses like Giunti, Ed. San Paolo, and DeAgostini, and in France, at Edition Jungle, Dargaud, and Drakoo. She is currently working on an unannounced project at Éditions Glénat. Ferarri often collaborates with Arancia Studio, an Italian creative media company.